Chelsea—A brainy **Alicia Silverstone** type with a southern twang, she's shocked by the tell-all topics of *Trash*. But by summer's end, *Trash* could be telling Chelsea's big secret!

Karma—This Asian beauty is a downtown Manhattan diva with **Fran Drescher**'s voice. Late nights? Cool clubs? Great shopping? Money to be made? Call Karma!

Lisha—Oh-so-cool, hotter than **Demi Moore**, they call her "Luscious Lisha" on the *Trash* set. She's not the same fat, awkward girl that Chelsea grew up with . . . is she?

Sky—Sweet, laid back, a T-shirt and jeans kind of guy who's a whiz with a movie camera, he gets mistaken a lot on the street for **Keanu Reeves** and is everyone's best bud.

Alan—This sensitive writer from Texas is sure the trash on *Trash* will give him tons of material. If **Johnny Depp** were a writer, he'd be Alan!

Nick—A Canadian slacker with a heart of gold. Chelsea's madly in love with this **Brad Pitt** double, but she has to wait in line behind their famous boss, Jazz Stewart!

Continued . . .

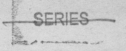

SERIES

the bosses

Jazz—The gorgeous **Daryl Hannah**-ish host of *Trash* is afraid of nothing, whether it's posing for nude pix on the beach in France, riding her Harley onto the set while clad in a bikini, or having three boyfriends at once. Because it's all *Trash*, isn't it?

Roxanne—The beautiful, icy, and ambitious associate producer, she's **Sharon Stone** at age twenty-something and loathes all interns on principle! Behind her back they call her "Bigfoot" . . . after those gigantic size-twelve dawgs!

Barry—The slick producer with the power, he's willing to help Chelsea go big places at *Trash*. The question is, is she willing to pay his price?

Sumtimes—Can a girl have a shaved head and still be gorgeous? Yes! The interns' fave producer got her nickname because she sometimes calls herself Cindy, sometimes Julia, sometimes *whatever*!

TRASH:
it's not just a job,
it's an adventure!

Cherie Bennett
and
Jeff Gottesfeld

BERKLEY BOOKS, NEW YORK

For Tammie Connors,
the coolest

TRASH

A Berkley Book / published by arrangement with
the authors

PRINTING HISTORY
Berkley edition / June 1997

The Putnam Berkley World Wide Web site address is
http://www.berkley.com/berkley

ISBN: 0-425-15851-9

BERKLEY®
Berkley Books are published by The Berkley Publishing Group,
200 Madison Avenue, New York, New York 10016.
BERKLEY and the "B" design
are trademarks belonging to Berkley Publishing Corporation.

PRINTED IN THE UNITED STATES OF AMERICA

10 9 8 7 6 5 4 3 2 1

"**M**y father was a mass murderer."

Chelsea Jennings took a shaky breath and leaned forward into the microphone.

"Did I forget to mention that? Maybe you've heard of him. Charles Kettering? That's right, the guy who went into the Burger Barn Restaurant in Johnson City, Tennessee, oh, about seventeen years ago, and shot every single person inside on one sunny Monday afternoon.

"Then he drove home—I mean, no one in the restaurant was left standing to stop him—and I guess his plan was to murder Mom, too—even though she did have his favorite lunch all ready for him on the dining-room table. Probably he planned to kill me, too—but, hey, I was only ten months old, so I don't really know.

"Anyway, Mom ended up killing Dad in-

1

stead—lucky for me, huh? And then, of course, Mom and me moved to Nashville, and changed our name, and then after that I really had a very normal life.

"Oh, and don't worry. I'm not much like him. I don't even have a bad temper—ha-ha.

"What else? Let's see. I'm valedictorian of my senior class. I'm a very hard worker. Oh, and I'm very interested in a future career in television. Which is why it means so much to me that you have hired me as a summer intern on your television show, *Trash*."

Chelsea put down her microphone—actually the hairbrush she had been *pretending* was a microphone—and stared at her reflection in the mirror over her dresser: shoulder-length golden-blond hair, large green eyes, all in all, a pretty, all-American-looking face gazing back at her. At the moment she was dressed in jeans, hiking boots, a man's white T-shirt with a beige suede vest over it, and a backward, gold-and-black Vanderbilt University baseball cap perched on her head.

Normal, she told herself. *I look totally normal. Like any other eighteen-year-old girl going off to New York City for her very first summer job as a TV intern.*

"It's a good thing being the only child of a psycho-killer doesn't show on your face," she told her reflection. "Of course, if you'd told them the truth, you'd probably be a guest on *Trash,* instead of an intern working for it."

No one knew the horrifying truth about her parents except her and her mother, and they never, ever talked about it. In fact, they both pretended that it had never really happened.

And most of the time, it doesn't seem as if it ever really did happen, Chelsea thought. *I can go days, weeks, sometimes even months, just living my life, hanging out with my friends, just normal me with my normal life.*

Except that my real name is Chelsea Kettering.

And up in the attic, hidden away, are the yellowed newspaper articles, the front-page headlines, about wealthy Johnson City attorney Charles Kettering, who just went bonkers one day and shot twenty-three people in a fast-food restaurant, and about his wife, Arlene, who stabbed her husband with a kitchen knife so he couldn't get to their innocent baby daughter.

And the front-page photos of me, the poor, innocent baby, wrapped in a white blanket with a duck on it, being carried out of the Ketterings' palatial home by some social worker.

Chelsea shook off her musings and picked up the glossy-covered folder that lay on her dresser, with the word TRASH on it in huge, raised neon letters. The folder had arrived in the mail a month earlier, and still Chelsea found it all somewhat hard to believe.

Chelsea's dream, every since she could remember, was to one day become a producer of some important television news show like *60 Minutes*. She had no desire to be in front of the camera—in fact, the very thought made her cringe. Rather, she wanted to be the one who made it all happen, who pulled the strings, uncovered corruption, spoke for the powerless, and hopefully made the world a better place.

Corny, but true, Chelsea thought. *And TV— really good TV—can do all that.*

However, Chelsea knew that thousands— even tens of thousands—of high-school grads wanted careers in TV, too. And she knew that many of them began by getting internships in the industry the same summer they graduated from high school.

An internship would be the all-important foot in the door, crucial if one had any hope at all of succeeding.

That's when Chelsea had come up with her game plan: she would spend three months of the fall of her senior year applying for every single TV internship in the entire country available to graduating high-school seniors. And then she'd be able to pick and choose among all the ones that offered her an internship.

So, she spent all her money from her after-school job at The Gap on postage and printing. She sent packets on herself everywhere, from prestigious shows like 60 *Minutes* (her dream) to the lowest-rated local TV station in Nashville. When she had exhausted all possibilities, her records showed she had applied for three hundred and forty-eight internships.

She was turned down by three hundred and forty-seven.

It was the biggest ego-bruiser of her life to date.

Oh, she'd been a finalist as an intern at a local station in Nashville, but she hadn't even gotten that.

It turned out that being the best and the brightest at her high school simply put her up against the best and the brightest from thousands of different high schools across America. In other words, she was utterly ordinary. Didn't stand out.

Didn't get picked.

Except by *Trash*.

Trash, of all places.

Trash was the number-one-rated talk show on TV. Geared to a Gen-X and teen audience, it was the most audacious show that had ever been on the airwaves. Frankly, Chelsea thought it was a pretty awful show, but she applied for the internship simply because she was applying for every single TV internship that existed.

Never in a million years did I think I had a shot, Chelsea thought. *And I still have absolutely no idea why they picked* me.

After all, on paper I look so normal, and Trash *is anything but! So what if I graduated number one in my class, and so what if I was editor of the Hume-Fogg Honors High School newspaper,* The Foghorn? *Those credentials* must be a big yawn, or else some other TV station or some other TV show would have offered me an internship.

But no one did.

She figured maybe it was the first-person essay she had written for her *Trash* application that had done the trick.

The directions had instructed her to "be wild and fearless, just like *Trash*."

So Chelsea had written her essay as if she was a teen runaway and drug addict, a prostitute on the streets, doing whatever she had to do for a fix.

And it wasn't until the end of the essay that she had admitted that none of it was true, but she added that she believed a real journalist should be willing to go anywhere and do anything to get a true story.

Yeah, like I'd really go live on the street and sleep with strange men and become a drug addict for a story, Chelsea thought. *I am the most clean-living, virginal, normal (or so* they *think), boring eighteen-year-old left in Nashville, Tennessee. And why* Trash *picked me when everyplace else in the entire country turned me down, I cannot imagine.*

But they did. And it's a famous show. And I'll get to live in New York. And I'll actually be working in TV. Hey, it's a foot in the door. It's a start. Thousands of kids didn't get picked at all.

Chelsea ran her fingers over the raised letters on the cover of her folder from *Trash,* then opened it and read, yet again, the tantalizing letter that was enclosed.

Dear Chelsea,

Congratulations!

Out of over ten thousand applicants, you have been selected as one of the six summer interns for *Trash,* the most controversial and hippest teen TV talk show in America today.

Rolling Stone calls us hipper than MTV's the *Real World. The New York Times* says we make Ricki Lake's show look like *Mr. Rogers' Neighborhood,* and our ratings prove that we are a national phenomenon, expressing the daring cutting edge of American youth today.

This summer, you will be a part of it.

Enclosed is all the information you will need regarding your housing in New York, job description, etc.

TRASH. EXCESS/ACCESS/SUCCESS.

Welcome aboard.

Barry Bassinger, Senior Producer

Chelsea flipped to the next page, which gave directions to the apartment on the Upper West Side of Manhattan that she would be sharing with the two other female *Trash* interns, only four blocks from the studios where *Trash* was aired daily in front of a live studio audience.

My own apartment, Chelsea rhapsodized. *And no mom there to have an anxiety attack if I'm five minutes late, or actually have a date with a guy she doesn't know, or—*

"Chelsea, honey?"

She quickly closed the folder and turned around. Her mother was standing in the doorway of her room, her face even more anxious looking than usual.

"Hi, Mom," Chelsea said, giving her mother a reassuring smile.

Her mother's eyes swept across Chelsea's packed suitcase and the small carry-on case with the rolled-up copy of *People* magazine sticking out. "So . . . all ready," her mother said, a slightly desperate edge to her voice.

"Please don't be upset, Mom—"

"I'm not," her mother assured even as she nervously patted her perfectly coiffed hair into place, which she always did when she was upset.

Chelsea tried to see her mother as a stranger might—the perfectly pressed navy pants and matching blazer, the understated strand of real pearls around her neck, the tasteful makeup on her attractive, unlined face.

Her mother always looked perfect. She taught music at an exclusive, private girls' school, she was on the board of a number of

8

charities, and she sang in the church choir. In fact, everything on the outside was always perfect—clothes, hair, home, daughter.

To hide what's going on inside, Chelsea knew. *To hide our horrible secret.*

"So, I guess we'd better leave for the airport," Chelsea said, picking up her purse and slinging the strap over her shoulder.

"New York is so far away. . . ." her mother began.

"It's going to be fine, Mom." She had been saying the exact same thing for a month, ever since she had received the letter in the mail telling her that she had actually, really and truly been picked for the *Trash* summer intern program.

"Well, I'm going to worry about you in that city, all by yourself," her mother insisted, her brow furrowed.

"I'll be fine," Chelsea said again. She picked up her suitcase and headed for the stairs.

"I still don't understand why you couldn't have accepted an internship from a nice show," her mother said, trailing behind her.

"Mom, this is an incredible opportunity," Chelsea maintained. She hadn't admitted to her mother that every other internship in the entire country had turned her down.

She had been too embarrassed.

"It's just that I've heard that *Trash* is just so . . . so . . . unsavory," her mother said, fiddling with her pearls. "I have friends who watch it. Evidently they have on drug addicts! And gang members. And homosexuals—"

"We have all that right here in Nashville, Mom," Chelsea said patiently.

"Well, perhaps so, dear," her mother replied, "but we don't associate with people like that."

Chelsea kissed her mother's cheek and started down the stairs. "We have to go, Mom."

Her mother hurried down the stairs after her. "Just remember, Chelsea, dear, that you're a well-brought-up young lady, won't you?"

"I will, Mom." Chelsea put her stuff in the back of the car, then got behind the wheel. Her mother got in the passenger seat.

"Because if you lie down with dogs, you get fleas," her mother added, clicking her seat belt in.

"Right," Chelsea said. "Dogs. Fleas."

"And you'll call me every night," her mother went on.

"If I can," Chelsea said absently, backing the car out of the driveway.

Her mother sighed, long and loud. "Well, it's only a summer. In the fall you'll be right back here at home, safe and sound. You'll go to Vanderbilt with the right sorts of girls and boys, and you'll make lovely new friends. Won't that be nice?"

Chelsea didn't reply. Just the thought of living at home for college and going to Vanderbilt with "the right sorts of girls and boys" felt like a noose tightening around her neck.

But maybe this summer will change every-thing, Chelsea thought as she pulled the car onto I-440 and hit the gas pedal. *Who knows? Maybe some miracle will occur and I won't have to come back here and go to Vanderbilt at all. . . .*

She felt hopeful. And scared. And daring. And on the edge of a million possibilities.

Ready for New York. Ready for anything.

So long as no one found out who she really was.

"I'm coming, I'm coming, keep your shirt on!" a nasal female voice with a definite New York accent called from inside the apartment.

From the other side of the door, Chelsea heard lock after lock turning, then a chain sliding, and finally the door opened as the head of a very pretty Asian girl, about Chelsea's age, peeked out.

She had gorgeous, long, straight black hair and wore lots of black eyeliner and very pale lipstick.

"Yeah?" the girl said in a guarded voice. "You're—?"

"Chelsea Jennings," Chelsea said, picking up her suitcase. "One of the *Trash* interns? Didn't the doorman downstairs just announce me?"

"Yeah, like that means anything," the girl said. Now she opened the door completely, and

13

Chelsea got a look at the rest of her. She was tiny, not much more than five feet tall, Chelsea figured. She had on ice-blue silk pants with a drawstring waist that fell below her navel, and a matching, cropped, ice-blue silk camisole.

The girl stepped aside and gestured Chelsea into the living room. "Honestly, you can't be too careful in this city. I'm Karma Kushner." She held out her hand for Chelsea to shake, then pointed at her. "Alicia Silverstone," she said.

"Pardon me?" Chelsea said.

"You look like that actress, Alicia Silverstone."

"Well, thanks," Chelsea said. "I mean, that's a nice compliment—"

"It's a thing I do," Karma said. "I look at people and decide what famous person they look most like. It drives my mother crazy. She looks like Anjelica Huston. 'Karma,' she always says, 'stop with the famous people look-alike bit!'"

"Your name is Karma—"

"Yeah, I know, it's bizarre," Karma agreed. "I mean, look at me, I'm Asian—I guess you noticed that—"

"Right off," Chelsea admitted.

"Yeah, right," Karma agreed. "And I have this, like, huggie-veggie first name and this Jewish last name, right? And, okay, I'm perfectly aware that I've got a voice like Fran Drescher on *The Nanny,* and you're like, 'What's up with that?' Am I right?"

"Kind of," Chelsea admitted.

"Jewish former-hippie parents," Karma explained. "I'm adopted. They own a New Age health food and bookstore now, out on Long Island. They're still in mourning over the end of the Age of Aquarius. Meanwhile I own twenty-three cashmere sweaters. I mean, they're, like, dying that they raised this materialistic daughter. So, come on, I'll show you around."

She picked up Chelsea's suitcase—which was almost as big as she was—and carried it through the living room and down a long narrow hallway. Chelsea glanced into a bedroom and glimpsed a beautiful mahogany canopy bed, and a bathroom with a shower curtain covered with nude Roman statues.

They turned into the third door on the right. It was a small furnished bedroom. The bedspread was bright pink, the bed was brass, the carpet a worn Oriental centered on a polished hardwood floor, and the wallpaper featured giant pink cabbage roses.

"I moved in two days ago," Karma said, "I couldn't wait to get out of Long Island. And frankly I took the best bedroom, with the canopy bed. This is the second best, if you can stomach Pepto-Bismol pink, which frankly is not one of my better colors. The other bedroom is tiny, but it has a water bed, in case you're into sex on the high seas."

"This is fine," Chelsea assured her. She felt both dazzled and a little shocked.

No one I know would talk about sex on a water bed, Chelsea thought.

Mom would just die, she added to herself, gleefully.

"So, listen," Karma said. "You wanna come out and gab? Because I've been dying for company. Or you need to put your stuff away?"

"I can do that later," Chelsea decided. "I didn't bring all that much, anyway."

"Smart," Karma said. "Because the shopping in New York is to die for. I know every great discount place for designer clothes. Come on, I'll make coffee."

Chelsea followed Karma out of the room and went into the living room while Karma went into the adjoining kitchen.

"I hope you like it really, really strong," Karma said, measuring out some coffee into the Mr. Coffee.

"Truthfully, I usually drink tea," Chelsea said.

"Oh, gag me," Karma snorted. "Reminds me too much of Mom and Dad. According to them, there's a tea for every occasion. Constipated? French vervain. Too aggressive? Camomile. Want to do past-life regression? There's a tea for it. Guaranteed."

Chelsea looked around the living room, trying to get acclimated. The furniture was old and substantial. She sat on a red velvet couch, shabby at the corners. A larger Oriental rug than the one in her bedroom covered most of the floor. The tables were dark brown and the lamps were old-fashioned and lace-covered.

Which made absolutely no sense when you looked at the artwork, which was modern, erotic, and, Chelsea thought, really, really bad.

"So, Chelsea, where are you from?" Karma asked as she got out two coffee cups. Clearly she had already learned where things were in the kitchen.

"Nashville, Tennessee," Chelsea replied. "You need help?"

"Nah," Karma said. "Yeah, you have a little accent. So, you ever been to New York before?"

"Never," Chelsea said. "I've always dreamed about it, though. And now I'm finally here. . . ." She stared at the painting behind the couch. It featured a naked woman standing on her head, balancing pianos on her feet. "The artwork in here is very strange," she said.

"It sucks," Karma said cheerfully, bringing in the coffee. "Can you believe how weird this apartment is? Old-lady furniture, and then a water bed in one bedroom, and this dreck on the walls?"

"I guess *Trash* rented it for us furnished," Chelsea said, sipping her coffee. She practically gagged, it was so strong.

"Yeah," Karma agreed. "But what I want to know is, who the hell furnished it?" She sat in the red velvet chair across from Chelsea and took a long swallow of her coffee.

"I live on this stuff," she continued. "I have

17

this night job I just started—bartending at this club in the East Village—it's called Jimi's—after Jimi Hendrix, ya know? The guy who owns the place's name is Arnold, which doesn't exactly ring a sexy bell, so I can see why he calls the place Jimi's." She took another sip of her coffee.

"Anyway," she continued, "I'm, like, doing a day job and a night job and I, like, live on caffeine. I should just do it intravenously!"

"Do you have to lie about your age to work there?" Chelsea asked. "Or are you older than eighteen—"

"Nah, I'm eighteen," Karma said. "I just graduated from South Long Island High School—that was three years of my life I'd sooner forget, thank you very much—but anyway, Jimi's is a teen club. No alcohol. They happen to be very hip at the moment. There's, like, this reverse thing happening with alcohol. It's really cool not to drink."

Chelsea nodded, as if all this information was normal to her. In actuality, her head was swimming and she felt overwhelmed. Clearly Karma loved to talk, though, so Chelsea didn't have to contribute too much for the time being.

"So, are you as psyched as I am about this *Trash* thing?" Karma asked. "I couldn't believe it when they picked me!"

"Me, neither," Chelsea agreed. "I mean, I feel like I'm so ordinary!"

"No one has ever described me as ordinary,"

Karma allowed, "but my grades in high school were so bad they barely let me graduate! I can't spell to save my life! God, I hope interns don't have to spell."

"You just use spell-check on the computer," Chelsea explained.

"Oh, yeah?" Karma said. "Great! Hey, you aren't one of those super-brains, are you?"

"Well, no—"

"Like one of those girls who got, like fifteen hundred on her SATs—"

"No . . ." Chelsea said carefully.

Karma eyed her. "You got higher. I can tell."

"Well . . ."

"You did," Karma accused. "What did you get?"

"Fifteen-sixty," Chelsea admitted meekly. "But I'm just one of those people who test well, and—"

"I'm dying here!" Karma whined. "Oh, my gawd, you are, like, *brilliant*!"

"Oh, I don't think I'm brilliant, I just—"

The buzzer next to the front door went off, loud and insistent,

"Our third roomie!" Karma cried, jumping up from her chair. "If she's another brain I'm killing myself." She pressed a black button on the wall and spoke into a small speaker. "Yeah?"

Static and noise came out of the speaker, followed by a garbled name neither girl could understand.

"Try again, Antoine," Karma called into the speaker.

More static and noise from the speaker.

"Yeah, sure, Antoine, have a nice day," Karma said into the speaker. "It could be a friggin' ax murderer and Antoine would send 'em up."

"He's the guy downstairs—?"

"Doorman," Karma said. "He stays up all night playing the trotters, he told me. Gonna hit it big and leave this job in the dust."

"Trotters?" Chelsea echoed.

"Yonkers Raceway? The horses? You got a lot to learn. . . ."

"And he actually told you that?" Chelsea asked.

"What can I say?" Karma shrugged. "People confide in me. Antoine suffers from serious sleep deprivation. And the intercom system is totally broken. Welcome to New York."

"Maybe we should report it to the manager of the building," Chelsea suggested. "And he'll see that it's fixed."

"Yeah, and maybe I'll find a Todd Oldham original at Woolworth's, but I doubt it," Karma said, draining her coffee.

Chelsea blushed and studied the bad art on the wall again, while Karma took the coffee cups into the small kitchen. "Hey, do you cook?"

"Not much," Chelsea admitted.

"Me, neither," Karma said. "Let's hope our

third roomie is the Galloping Gourmet, or we'll be living at the Greek diner on the corner."

The doorbell rang, and Karma went through her who-is-it routine at the door again. Of course the response was unintelligible, but Karma unlocked the locks, undid the chain, and opened the door anyway.

"So, what we wanna know is, can you cook?" she asked the girl.

Chelsea couldn't see her, since Karma was standing in front of the door.

"I can boil water," came a throaty reply, "but I only do it under duress."

"We're screwed," Karma said cheerfully, ushering the new girl into the apartment. "I'm Karma Kushner, by the way." She turned to look at me, pointing at the new girl. "Demi Moore," she pronounced, "but younger."

The new girl walked in and looked around, and Chelsea studied her. She had short, shaggy brown hair that fell sexily over her forehead, into her large, almond-shaped blue eyes. She wore a pair of teeny tiny cutoffs and a sleeveless black T-shirt, and black boots that laced almost up to her knees. Chelsea could see the outline of a tattoo on her shoulder, though she couldn't make out what it was. The girl was utterly confident, curvy, sexy, and cool.

And totally intimidating.

All she carried was a shabby backpack, which she dropped in the center of the living-room floor.

"Wow, weird," the girl said, looking around at the conservative furniture and the bad erotic art.

Something about her is familiar, Chelsea mused, *something about her voice. . . .*

"What's with the tacky art?" the girl asked in her throaty, sexy voice, making a face at the upside-down nude.

"We wondered, too," Chelsea said.

And then, for the first time, the new girl looked at Chelsea. Really looked at her. She blinked slowly. "No," she said. "It can't be."

"Pardon me?" Chelsea asked, taken aback.

The new girl stared at her for another beat, and then she laughed.

"She's laughing," Karma commented as she shut the door. "I didn't hear a joke, but the girl clearly finds something hilarious."

"It's a pretty good joke, too," the girl said, her hands shoved into the tight pockets of her cut-offs. She looked right at Chelsea. "You don't recognize me?"

Chelsea studied her. "I'm sorry. I mean, if we've met before, I guess I don't remember. Your voice sounds familiar, but—"

"It should," the girl said. She took a step toward Chelsea. "You're Chelsea."

Chelsea's heart thudded in her chest. *Oh, God, please don't let this be my worst nightmare come true,* she thought. *Please don't let this be someone who knows the truth about me. No. I'm being paranoid. No one knows. It can't be—*

22

"Chelsea," the girl said, taking her hands out of her pockets. "It's Alyssa."

Now it was Chelsea's turn to stare. Alyssa *Bishop*? Alyssa Bishop had been Chelsea's best friend all through grade school and junior high, but then she and her family had moved to Denver, and after about six months of letter writing, they had lost touch with each other.

But this couldn't be Alyssa. Alyssa was overweight, with an overbite that made her top teeth stick out. She was shy and quiet, and an excellent student.

But even if some kids thought Alyssa was kind of geeky, Chelsea knew how smart and funny and irreverent Alyssa really was, how she was the most fun person in the world to be with, how she could make anything exciting. She wasn't the lump her parents or the other kids thought she was at all. In fact, behind her thick glasses were the sparkling, mischievous blue eyes of—

Chelsea stared into the new girl's eyes.

Blue. So blue. Just like Alyssa's. And the voice, the funny, froggy, sexy voice that didn't seem to go with the plump, funny-looking little girl at all . . .

"Alyssa Bishop?" Chelsea whispered.

"It's really me," the girl said. "Only everyone calls me Lisha now."

"But . . . you changed," Chelsea managed.

Lisha laughed. "You didn't."

23

And the next thing they knew, they were hugging and laughing and crying, all at the same time.

"I love happy endings," Karma said, "but I feel like I missed the first reel of the movie here."

Chelsea broke away from Lisha, a huge grin on her face. "We were best friends when we were kids," Chelsea explained. "But Alyssa moved to Denver—"

"And I changed, thank God," Lisha added. "I used to be fat—"

"You?" Karma asked incredulously. "I would kill to have a body like yours. I have to practically buy my clothes in the children's department."

"Believe me, I was a lump," Lisha said. "And I had this overbite, and glasses. . . ."

"But you were always wonderful," Chelsea said. "I missed you so much when you moved away. . . . God, I just can't believe this!"

"Me, either," Lisha said. She shook her head in wonder. "This is really out there. What are the odds that the two of us would both get picked to be interns at *Trash*?"

"Slim to none," Chelsea said. She felt as if her mouth would break from smiling so hard. "I want to hear about everything that's happened to you!"

"Oh, this means I need to make more coffee," Karma announced. "Hey, I hope you like water beds," she added to Lisha as she hurried into the kitchen.

"Depends on who's in it with me," Lisha said. She sat on the couch. So did Chelsea. "So, tell me—"

There was a knock on the door.

"Who's that?" Karma asked. "The doorman didn't buzz us."

Chelsea and Lisha just shrugged.

Another knock.

"We could buzz down to Antoine," Karma suggested. "Not that he'd be conscious enough to offer an opinion."

"Let's just open the door," Lisha said, getting up from the couch.

"Oh, sure," Karma said sarcastically, hurrying across the room. "And if any of us could cook we could invite Freddy Kreuger out there to dinner. He'd supply the fresh meat."

She stood on tiptoe so she could see through the peephole in the door. "Who is it?" she yelled.

"Ick!" came a male voice.

"Okay, there's a guy standing at our door yelling 'ick.' I can't see a thing through the stupid peephole. What do we do?"

Lisha strode over to the door. "Who?" she called.

"Nick!" the voice yelled.

Karma shrugged. "So kill me. It sounded like 'ick' to me."

Lisha looked through the peephole. "There's

more than one guy out there," she said. "In fact, it looks like three," she reported. "I'm opening the door."

"Are you on drugs?" Karma screeched. "This is New York! You can't just—"

The door was open. Chelsea and Karma both peered around Lisha to see who was there.

It was, as reported, three guys.

Three *cute* guys.

Three *incredibly* cute guys.

"Hi," the one standing in the front with the Brad Pitt blue eyes and dirty-blond ponytail said. "I'm Nick Shaw. This is Alan Van Kleef and Sky Addison," he added, cocking his head toward the two guys with him.

One had dark hair and a sensitive, finely chiseled face, and the other had short brown hair and the lean, muscular body of a serious athlete.

"We're the other three *Trash* interns," Nick explained. He gave a dazzling smile.

"And we live right across the hall."

3

"So, you got it?" the assistant producer, Cindy Sumtimes, asked Chelsea, her voice harried. She looked down at the three wristwatches on her left wrist, saw the time, and swore under her breath.

"Yes," Chelsea said tentatively, "I think so. I mean—"

"You can't *think so,*" Cindy said, as if Chelsea was the slowest, most annoying kid on the block, "you have to *know so.*"

She checked her watches again, then ran her hand nervously over her entirely shaved scalp. Her eyebrows were shaved off, too, and new eyebrows drawn on. But Cindy Sumtimes was so beautiful that she actually managed to look good anyway.

"Listen . . . Chutney, was it?"

"Chelsea," Chelsea said politely.

"Yeah," Cindy said distractedly. She pulled

up a folding chair and slid onto it backward, her legs splayed. "Because if you screw this up, Jazz'll eat me alive. All you have to do is—"

Riiiiiing. Riiiiiiiing.

It was a tiny mobile phone that Cindy wore tucked into the oversized pocket of her hot-pink leather overalls.

"Sumtimes," Cindy barked her last name into the phone. "Yeah . . . uh-huh . . ."

As Cindy began pacing the office with the phone, Chelsea's mind wandered.

It was her first day of work at *Trash*—actually, Chelsea's first hour on the job. She'd hardly been able to get to sleep the night before, she had been so revved up—a combination of excited and exhilarated—and also very, very nervous.

Imagine me, Chelsea Jennings, working in television, she thought to herself, for maybe the hundredth time. *So what if it's* Trash—*it's national TV! I'll make great connections that can launch my career. I'll meet famous people. I'll learn all about how television really works.*

I'll work with incredibly cute guy interns.

And they're so nice, Chelsea thought, smiling dreamily. *Really, really nice guys.*

When they had arrived in New York, neither she, Karma, nor Lisha had known that the guy interns for *Trash* were going to be housed right across the hall from them. The night before, they had all ordered in Chinese food—so much better than any Chelsea had ever tasted in

28

Nashville—and it had been delivered by a young Asian guy on a bicycle!

Chelsea had eaten squid for the first time—actually, Nick had bet her that she wouldn't eat it and then he had actually fed her a pink, dangly, icky-looking piece, dropping it into her mouth from between two chopsticks, and then—

"Yo, Chutney?" Cindy said, standing over her. "Can we focus here?"

"Sorry," Chelsea replied, embarrassed, turning her attention back to the task that the producer had outlined for her. She didn't want to tell Cindy yet again what her name really was.

"So let me repeat it for you," Cindy said slowly, tapping her fingers on the desk. "This is the expert file. Jazz wants each expert's name, address, phone, and specialty on a separate *Trash* index card."

"The cards go in the box," Chelsea recited, pointing to an enormous case on the floor by her side, filled with four-by-six-inch index cards, in colors ranging from pale yellow to deep purple, all with the distinctive *Trash* logo printed on the back.

"That's right," Cindy said, nervously checking her watches again. "Keep it alphabetical, and make each expert's specialty a separate color. You've got ten thousand cards and a hundred fifty colors, so you should be all set."

"And I take the information off the computer," Chelsea said, indicating the screen in front of her.

"You got it," Cindy said. "Okay, I gotta run, Jazz'll kill me if I'm late. Okay, if you need me, it's extension three-four-one, Sumtimes."

"Thanks, Cindy," Chelsea said politely.

But Cindy was already gone, on a dead run to somewhere or other, leaving behind only the scent of some great perfume.

Chelsea looked at the huge pile of cards on the floor and sighed. *Well, okay, so it's a weenie job,* she thought. *But, after all, I have to expect that some of the stuff I do is going to be boring. I mean, I'm only an intern.*

For now.

But someday . . . someday I'll be a big producer, she dreamed, *on some fantastic show like* 60 Minutes. *I'll uncover corruption and travel all over the world, I'll make a fortune, I'll win the Pulitzer Prize for journalism, and they'll do a profile on me for* People *magazine . . .*

. . . And some young, hungry reporter will dig for the dirt about me, and she'll find out who I really am.

Oh, God . . .

Chelsea dropped her head into her hands. *You have to stop this,* she told herself. *You've never in your whole life spent time obsessing about what happened with your parents. You've always ignored it and pretended it never happened, and now is not the time to change things!*

Chelsea got up and looked around the office.

The gold nameplate on the large Lucite desk read BARRY BASSINGER, SENIOR PRODUCER. The large office featured all modern, beige suede furniture that sat on beige carpeting so thick that Chelsea's steps felt springy when she walked. A huge window gave a view of the street scene below.

Chelsea walked over to the wall closest to the window, where a series of photos hung.

I guess that's Barry, Chelsea thought, since the same small, dark-haired, good-looking guy, about thirty-five, Chelsea guessed, was featured in each photo.

In one photo he had his arm around Madonna. In another he was on a boat with a bikini-clad Cindy Crawford in his lap. And in another Sandra Bullock was kissing his cheek.

"Where's Barry?"

Chelsea swung around guiltily. A tall, handsome Hispanic guy with gorgeous hair that hung halfway down his back stood in the doorway.

"I—I don't know," Chelsea stammered, her face red. She felt as if she had been caught looking through drawers or something.

"I got papers for him," the guy said impatiently, waving a bunch of papers in his hand.

"I guess you can put them on his desk," Chelsea said with a shrug.

"You his new secretary?" the guy asked, flipping his gorgeous hair over his shoulders.

"Oh, no, I'm—"

"Didn't think so," the guy said, crossing to the Lucite desk and dropping the papers. "You're not the type." He strode back to the door and slammed it on his way out.

"I feel like Alice in Wonderland," Chelsea murmured out loud. "People just keep coming and going. . . ."

She looked down at the outfit she'd so carefully chosen for the first day of work, and wondered what the guy had meant by "you're not the type."

Chelsea had spent an hour that morning trying to figure out the best thing to wear, and had tried on practically everything in her meager wardrobe. She hadn't lied when she'd told Karma that she hadn't brought much, but it wasn't because she planned to shop in New York. It was because she didn't own much. Her mother didn't make very much money teaching at a private school, and Chelsea had earned money for her clothes at her after-school job at The Gap at the Bellevue Mall.

The Gap discount was a huge help. Just about all of her clothes were from that store. Today she had on a pair of black cotton trousers and a white muslin collarless shirt. Her hair was tied back with a black ribbon, and she wore flat, men's-looking oxford shoes on her feet.

Businesslike, but cute, she had thought to herself that morning, adding some mascara to her blond eyelashes.

She had felt confident about her choice, until Karma and Lisha walked out of their bedrooms that morning.

Lisha had on a pair of baggy, faded jeans that rode low on her hipbones. With this she wore the top of a Cub Scout uniform, tied under her bust. The merit badge on her shoulder was for wildlife.

Karma had on a red felt poodle skirt, circa 1950s, only whereas poodle skirts usually came down to the calves, Karma's was mid-thigh. With it she wore a tiny, sleeveless white mohair vest and very high heels.

"Wow, you guys look nice," Chelsea had managed.

"You, too," they had both told her.

But now she knew they were just being nice. Because everyone at *Trash* seemed to have this wild sense of fashion. No one looked like anyone else.

And clearly no one else here but me shops at The Gap.

I guess I'm the token boring-looking person, Chelsea thought with a sigh, fiddling with a button on her white blouse.

The buzzer on the Lucite desk went off, startling her. She hurried over to the desk and picked up the phone, as Cindy Sumtimes had instructed her to do.

"Barry Bassinger's office," Chelsea said into the phone, her voice sounding thin and nervous in her own ears. "Chelsea Jennings speaking."

"How many?" the voice on the phone barked.

"Excuse me?" Chelsea said, bewildered.

"I said how many," the voice repeated irritably, and now Chelsea recognized it as Cindy Sumtimes. "How many cards have you done by now?"

"Uh, well, uh . . ." Chelsea stammered, embarrassed that she'd been daydreaming for the past ten minutes. "Not too many yet . . ."

"Look, Chutney, get to it!" Cindy yelled, then she hung up.

Chelsea hung up the receiver and turned to the task she'd been assigned.

I mean, the whole assignment is so pointless, she thought. *It's so much easier to access this information on computer, and if Jazz wants a printout, it can just be printed out and put on cards.*

I said that to Cindy, Chelsea remembered. *And Cindy looked at me like I was crazy. And then she said, "If Jazz had said that she wanted this stuff handwritten on file cards while you're standing on your head, you'd be upside down right about now. Understood?"*

She stared at the list on the computer.

There were hundreds of topics, ranging from Animals (teens who have killed or mutilated) to Yacking (teens who can't stop). And everything in between. Most of which seemed to deal with either sex, drugs, alcohol, or crime.

Chelsea sighed one more time and, beginning with Animals, dutifully began transposing the data onto file cards. It was excruciatingly boring work, but she vowed that these were going to be the very best file cards that Jazz had ever had put into her hands.

She worked for two hours straight before she stopped to stand up and stretch her legs. Idly, she walked over to the window and looked out. The offices and studio of *Trash* were located in a building overlooking the Hudson River, and because it was such a warm June day, there were many pleasure boats on the river.

Last night Sky said that his uncle captains a fishing boat, Chelsea recalled. She could just picture Sky's open and friendly face, his large brown eyes and strong jawline.

He's so nice and sweet, Chelsea thought. *He's even in the Big Brother program in Brooklyn, and he showed us pictures of his family. He's interested in the tech stuff, like camera work, and I guess it didn't hurt that his dad is really big in the TV tech union when he applied to be an intern here.*

And he's so cute. Karma says he's teenage Keanu Reeves. He's so nice, so easy to talk to, I feel like he could have been one of my buds from high school, and—

"Hey!"

Chelsea turned around.

As if she had willed it, Sky Addison had stuck his head in the door. "How ya doing?"

"Hi!" Chelsea said, happy to see a friendly face. She walked over to him. "How did you know I was in here?"

"Karma told me," Sky reported. "I ran into her in the Xerox room. She already seems to know where everything and everyone is. So, how's it going?"

"Well, to tell you the truth, it's basically boring," Chelsea admitted. "I'm writing things on file cards. What have they got you doing?"

"Well, first I Xeroxed papers for the audio engineer—I have no idea what they were—and now I'm on my way to the control room, to learn how the cameras work."

"Lucky you," Chelsea said enviously.

"Well, keep your chin up," Sky said. "Don't let 'em drown you in file cards!" He flashed his great grin again and left.

He's definitely the friendliest of the three guy interns, Chelsea thought as she forwarded the computer to more experts' names.

Now Alan Van Kleef—Johnny Depp, according to Karma—is the most sensitive, Chelsea mused, picking up a tangerine-colored index card. *He wants to be a writer. Last night he told us that his dad was really disappointed in him because he didn't want to work in the family business. And I bet there are a lot of sons out there who would want to work in the family business, if their dad owned a National Football League team like Alan's dad does! But Alan thought that working on* Trash *would give him good material for a book.*

Chelsea looked up at the computer screen. She was up to the Cs—Cannibals (teens who claim to have eaten human flesh). She shuddered at the thought.

That has to be made up, she decided. *Half the stuff in here had to be made up.* She reached for another index card, and her mind wandered off again.

To Nick. Nick Shaw.

Her heart jumped, just thinking his name in her mind.

He's Brad Pitt. Definitely Brad Pitt.

Chelsea had been so attracted to him the night before that it was hard for her even to be around him. She had felt breathless and tongue-tied, stupid and flushed.

I hope no one noticed, she thought. *God, that would be so totally humiliating.*

And what is his deal, anyway? Chelsea thought, the sky-blue index card in front of her blurring. *He's a total slacker, as far as I can tell. Last night he was wearing jeans and a huge flannel shirt, and today he's wearing exactly the same thing.*

Chelsea smiled and closed her eyes, images of Nick dancing in her mind. *I like the fact that a guy that fine isn't into his looks,* she thought. *It's like he's not even aware of how impossibly hot he is. Even though he is so hot that . . .*

She opened her eyes. *No. I am not the kind of girl who falls for some guy just because he's hot.*

"But it's more than that," she murmured out loud, as if she were having an argument with herself. *When I talked—Lisha and Karma, too, for that matter—Nick really listened,* she recalled. *So many great-looking guys just pretend to listen to girls, some fake the Mr. Sensitive thing, meanwhile all they're really thinking about is getting your clothes off. . . .*

Not Nick. I can tell.

Or maybe it's Belch, she thought, smiling at the memory of Nick's mongrel dog, whom he had brought over later in the evening the night before. *Belch is the cutest, coolest dog I ever met in my life.*

And he can belch on command. Nick said "belch," and he—

The phone rang again. Chelsea answered right away.

It was Cindy. "How many?" she barked into the phone. "How many cards?"

Chelsea took a quick look at the table in front of her. She'd organized the piles of file cards into piles of ten, and there were thirteen piles on Barry's desk, along with three cards directly in front of her, in the category of Cross-Dressers (Teen).

"I've done one hundred and thirty-three," Chelsea said hesitantly.

Silence on the phone.

"Is that okay?" Chelsea asked anxiously.

"Yeah, not bad," Cindy allowed. "So, take a coffee break. The staff lounge is the third door on the left when you turn right out of Barry's office. I'll stop by and check your work while you're there."

Once again, Cindy hung up the phone without saying good-bye.

"Coffee break, right," Chelsea mumbled as she made her way down the hallway to the *Trash* employees' lounge.

The room was a disaster. Half-consumed foam cups of coffee lay on a scarred wooden table. Some stale-looking jelly doughnuts spilled out of a box on the counter. Someone had left a half-eaten bagel on the lumpy orange tweed couch. Above that a bulletin board overflowed with haphazardly placed notices, notes, and photos.

"It's a total dump," Karma said as Chelsea took in the disaster of the room.

Karma was sitting on the couch, holding a photocopied article from some newspaper in her hands. She had kicked off her high heels and her feet were up on a small gold vinyl footrest with the stuffing coming out of it. "Why didn't you stop me from wearing these shoes this morning?" Karma whined. "My feet are killing me."

"So don't wear them tomorrow," Chelsea said, pouring herself a cup of the thick-looking coffee.

"It's the worst," Karma said, indicating the coffee. "Swill. I gotta bring in better stuff."

"So, what have you been doing?" Chelsea asked. She took a sip of the coffee. Karma was right. It was vile.

"Oh, you know, glamorous stuff," Karma said in her nasal whine. "I filed papers. I answered a phone." She thrust the photocopied page she had been reading at Chelsea. "You gotta read this."

It was an article photocopied from that morning's *New York Daily News*.

TRASH'S JAZZ STEWART SET FOR BARBARA WALTERS TELEVISION SPECIAL

Jazz Stewart, the white-hot, white-blond, nineteen-year-old host of the TV-talk-show phenomenon *Trash,* has been invited by television interviewer Barbara Walters to join her in a half-hour-long, one-on-one special, to be broadcast over the Labor Day weekend.

Stewart's story, and her rise from being a sexy dancer on an afternoon music-video channel's teen dance show to being the cover story of last week's *People* magazine, is well-known.

"We want to go beyond the brains and the great legs," one of Walters's producers said, "and we want to make this daughter of rock-and-roll groupie Pamela Brewer real to our viewers. No one can do it like Barbara can."

Stewart, who claims to be the illegitimate daughter of Rod Stewart, has had her show for only nine months, but, in syndication, it has penetrated every major television market in the USA, and has achieved higher ratings in a shorter time than any other talk show in history.

Accompanying the article was a quarter-page photo of Jazz, taken on the beach at Saint-Tropez, France, last month.

In it, Jazz was wearing nothing but the world's tiniest bikini bottom and a sultry sneer, her arms crossed across her breasts.

"She's a sluttier-looking Daryl Hannah," Karma decreed, looking at the photo over Chelsea's shoulder. "Gawd, I would kill to have Jazz's body."

"Why bother?" Lisha said, striding in the open door to the lounge. Evidently she had overheard Karma's comment. "I mean, you, too, could buy those body parts at your friendly neighborhood plastic surgeon's."

"What, you're telling me she had a boob job?" Karma asked, squinting at the photo.

"I heard she had an *everything* job," Lisha said, pouring herself some coffee. "So, how's life in the fast lane, you guys?"

"We did secretarial stuff," Chelsea said, still studying Jazz's photo. "Do you really think she's had plastic surgery? I mean, she's only nineteen!"

"Who'd you hear this dish from?" Karma demanded.

"What difference does it make?" Lisha asked. "Jazz did what she needed to do. And now she's hot."

"And we work for her," Karma added, "which makes us very, very warm."

"Right," Lisha agreed, making a face at the vile coffee. "Which is why when Jazz tells us to jump, we will say 'how high?'"

The phone on the table next to Chelsea rang loudly.

Is there anyplace in this office that is less than ten feet from a phone? Chelsea thought, automatically reaching to pick it up.

"Uh, employees' lounge, Chelsea Jennings speaking," she said, hoping she was answering the phone the right way.

"Why didn't you tell me your name was Chelsea?" Cindy barked into the phone. "I've been walking around calling you Chutney all morning!"

"Well, I—"

"Glad to see you found the lounge. Listen, is Karma and what's-her-name—the other intern—"

"Lisha," Chelsea said.

"Right," Cindy agreed. "They both in there?"

"Yes," Chelsea replied.

"Well, cool," Cindy said. "I've got a little surprise for you guys. Why don't you come down to the set? Barry wants you guys to see an actual taping in progress. Usually we air live, with a six-second delay, but Jazz wants some shows in the can for when she goes on vacation."

Cindy hung up. No good-bye, but Chelsea was used to it by now.

"We've been summoned," Chelsea said, getting up from the couch.

"All of us?" Lisha asked.

Chelsea nodded. "We're supposed to go to the set. I think we're about to find out exactly why *Trash* is the trashiest hit of all time!"

"Ladies, ladies, ladies!" a short, slight guy in faded jeans and a Nine Inch Nails T-shirt called out as Chelsea, Lisha, and Karma entered through the side door of Studio C.

Studio C hadn't been easy to find. And once they had found it, they had to give their names to a monitor, who stood just outside the door. A sign over the door read LIVE, but as the girls entered, it was not lit up.

"I'm Barry Bassinger, senior producer," the guy said, a warm smile on his face. "You met Sumtimes this morning, right?"

Next to him, in the rear of the room, Cindy Sumtimes waggled her fingers at the girls, her eyes on the technicians moving cameras around the stage area.

Chelsea took it all in, wide-eyed. She recognized the *Trash* set from what she'd seen on TV, although she was surprised to find that it was much smaller than it looked on the tube.

But there was the infamous *Trash* logo painted on the nude, faux-marble statue of David. There was the comfortable overstuffed furniture, the wooden coffee table, the inflatable man now lolling on the couch with a top hat hanging over his crotch, the inflatable woman hanging upside down from a curtain.

And every show, the inflatable people hang somewhere else, Chelsea recalled, thrilled in spite of her general dislike for the show. It was all just so . . . so magical and seductive.

And there, on the coffee table, is the bowl of M&M's that Jazz always eats. I've seen it all so many times on TV, but now I'm really, truly here. I actually work here!

"Hey, Sumtimes!" a woman wearing white go-go boots and a lime-green micro-mini called as she ran over to them. "We got a problem with today's shrink."

"What, a hair problem?" Cindy asked.

"Well, her hair looks like dog meat," the other woman said. "But also she's wearing houndstooth, which, as you know, will go all blurry on camera. Plus she claims she's allergic to all cosmetics, so she won't let José touch her face with a makeup brush."

"Geez, just what I need, a neurotic shrink," Cindy said with disgust, getting up from her chair. "Lemme see her."

They hurried off together.

"So, who's who?" Barry asked.

They quickly introduced themselves.

"Great, great," Barry said. "So, you're about to see your first *Trash* show. Remember our motto: Excess, Access, Success!"

"Okay, Mack, let 'em in!" a guy with earphones on called from the stage.

At that moment, as if they were in a marathon and someone had just shot off the starter pistol, throngs of people swarmed into the studio. The quickest—or rudest—elbowed their way to the front and claimed seats.

"Brenda! Over here!" a skinny, sallow-faced teenage girl in a sweatshirt featuring a puffy pink kitten called to the back of the room.

"Excuse me," said the Hispanic guy that Chelsea had seen earlier, coming over to the girl. "The front seats are reserved. You need to sit back there."

"I don't see no sign that says that!" the girl exclaimed huffily.

"And yet it's true," he said.

He looked the audience over, moving people around, some to the front and some to the back.

"Why is he doing that?" Chelsea asked.

"I know," Lisha said, watching the audience reseating continue. "He's moving the hip, good-looking people to the front, because they'll be on camera more, right?"

Barry grinned at her. "Smart girl," he approved. "So, this is how it works. Roxanne or Demetrius—he's the dude over there who looks

47

like a Spanish superhero—the one with the hair—and Roxanne you'll see later on—one of them will warm up the audience. Then Jazz will come out—the audience always goes wild, of course—and we go live, and we're happening!"

Chelsea looked over the buzzing audience. They were all young, she realized, and there was a reason for that. No one over the age of thirty was allowed in the studio audience. ID was checked at the door.

"What's the subject of today's show?" Karma asked.

"Transvestite Teen Girls versus Real Teen Girls—who's sexier?" Barry recited.

"You mean guys who dress up like girls versus real girls?" Chelsea asked, wanting to make sure she knew what he meant.

"You got it," Barry said. "Sumtimes took them shopping yesterday. We dropped a bundle at Victoria's Secret. One guy had to have two corsets sewn together to get something that would fit him."

"Gee . . ." Chelsea said, at a loss for words.

Barry smiled at her. "Where you from?"

"Nashville," Chelsea admitted. She felt utterly provincial, standing there in her little Gap outfit.

"Oh yeah, right," Barry said. "I remember that from your application. Let's see. You want a career in TV, something serious," he continued. "You probably read classics for fun. Am I right?"

Chelsea blushed at being so transparent.

"Hey, it's cool," Barry said easily. "Just remember that more people's lives are affected by pop culture than have ever read *Ethan Frome*."

"Good," Karma said, "because I was forced to read that book my junior year and I, like, totally hated it."

Barry laughed. He turned to Lisha. "How about you? You an intellectual, too?"

Lisha shrugged and eyed him coolly.

How does she get away with that? Chelsea wondered. *It's like nothing in the whole world intimidates her. How did she change so much between junior high and now?*

"Okay, we're set down here," Demetrius said into his headphones. "Who's doing the warm-up, me or Roxanne?"

Chelsea could hear because there was a set of headphones on the chair where Cindy Sumtimes had been sitting.

"Roxi," the guy in the booth said. "She's on her way."

At that moment the curtain at the side of the stage parted, and an incredible-looking girl walked out onto the set. She was very tall and thin, with sexy red hair that fell over one eye, and cheekbones so high you could serve dinner off of them. She wore a perfect white designer suit with a very, very short skirt. Underneath

49

the jacket she wore nothing but her perfect, creamy skin.

No one in the audience knew who she was, but she was clearly *someone,* and their excited conversations dropped off expectantly.

"Hello," the girl said coolly. "I'm Roxanne Renault."

"Uh-uh," Karma whispered to Chelsea. "She's Sharon Stone with red hair."

"Welcome to *Trash,*" Roxanne continued. "As you know, the audience is a major part of our show. You'll be on live, which means that all of America is about to see you and hear you."

The audience tittered their excitement to each other.

"Ask lots of questions," Roxanne continued. "Don't be afraid to be outrageous. After all, that's what we're known for. There's nothing you can't do or say on *Trash.*"

"Don't mention that to the censors," Barry whispered to the girls.

"How does that work?" Chelsea whispered back as Roxanne continued her spiel down front.

"We're on a six-second delay," Barry explained. "They try to bleep out anything that doesn't live up to FCC standards. They fail a lot."

"So, now," Roxanne continued, "to get you into the *Trash* frame of mind, we're going to make two of you into superstars." Her eyes scanned the audience. Hands flew into the air, even though, as far as Chelsea knew, they had no idea in the world what they might be volunteering for.

"You," Roxanne said, pointing to the girl in the puffy-print sweatshirt who now sat near the back of the studio, "and you." She pointed to a very overweight girl in bulging stretch leopard-print pants.

The two girls eagerly came down on to the stage.

"Would you like to win some money?" Roxanne asked them in her purring voice.

"Sure!" Puffy Print exclaimed.

"Uh-huh," the other girl agreed eagerly. She waved to someone in the back of the room.

"Okay," Roxanne said.

Demetrius and Alan Van Kleef pushed a large box on wheels—about eight feet by eight feet—out on to the stage. It appeared to be filled with mud.

"There are ten twenty-dollar bills hidden in that box of mud," Roxanne said. "All you two ladies have to do is to jump in and mud-wrestle for one minute. Whoever is left standing, gets all the money."

Puff Print jumped up and down with excitement. The other girl looked reluctant.

"Oh, come on," Roxanne coaxed her. "This is *Trash*. You have to get into the spirit of the show, right?"

"I guess," the heavy young woman agreed.

"Cool," Roxanne said, smiling. "Oh, and one other thing. We have outfits for you to wear while you're wrestling—we wouldn't want you to get your nice clothes all messed up. Just step backstage and an assistant will give them to you."

Dutifully, the two girls walked offstage.

"They're really going to mud-wrestle for money?" Chelsea asked dubiously.

"Yeah," Barry confirmed. "This is one of our tamer warm-ups."

Roxanne talked to the audience for two more minutes, and then the two teen girls came back out onto the stage.

They were both wearing pig outfits.

"Okay, you two little oinkers!" Roxanne said gaily. "Go for it!"

This is just so humiliating, Chelsea thought. *I feel so embarrassed for those girls.*

But evidently the girls didn't share Chelsea's sensibilities. They eagerly got into the box of mud and went at each other. Over a sound system came a singsong version of "The Farmer in the Dell."

The audience cracked up, and the girls in the mud box got more and more into it, falling, sliding, hurling mud at each other.

After a minute of this "hilarity," a gong went off.

"Time for the audience to vote," Roxanne said. She held her hand over the skinny girl, and there was polite applause. Then she held her hand over the fat girl, who egged the audience on for more accolades, and the audience went wild.

"You win!" Roxanne said as the two girls climbed out of the mud box. "Did you have fun?"

"Oh, yeah!" the skinny girl said enthusiastically, wiping some mud out of her eye. "I coulda whipped her butt if we'd gone longer."

"Well, go backstage and someone cute with bulging muscles will hose you down," Roxanne promised. She turned to the heavy girl. "You get all the money," she told her.

"Great!" the girl said happily, wiping some mud off her eye.

"Of course, you have to dive back in the mud pit and dig for it," Roxanne added.

The audience hooted at this turn of events, and the heavy girl's face fell.

"Hey, just kidding!" Roxanne said gaily. She turned to the audience. "How about a nice hand for a good sport?"

The audience applauded dutifully and the girl walked offstage, waving to the studio audience as they left.

"And now," Roxanne said, her voice reverential, "the person you've all been waiting for. Please welcome . . . Jazz!"

The audience came roaring to its feet, screaming and cheering with excitement.

Nothing happened.

The stage was empty.

And then, over the roar of the audience, came the sound of a motor. A Harley motor, revving.

Jazz roared onto the stage, on a huge chopper. She was dressed all in black leather, from head to foot. She parked the bike in the center of the set and pulled off her helmet. Her gorgeous, trademark white-blond hair came flying around her incredible face.

"Don't you hate it when people tell you what to do?" she asked the audience without preamble.

"Yeahhhhh!" the young audience cheered.

"And don't you hate it when people tell you what you should be?" Jazz went on.

"Yeahhhh!" the audience cheered, even louder.

"I can't hear you," Jazz said, giving the audience a look that told them they had disappointed her.

"Yeahhhhh!" they screamed as one.

"Again," Jazz commanded.

"Yeahhhhhh!" they screamed again.

"Live from New York," a deep male voice said over a sound system, "it's *Trash!*"

The applause sign lit up and the audience went wild, yelling and screaming, jumping out of their seats. As they did this Jazz slowly and wordlessly began to strip out of her black leather, as hot rock and roll blared over the sound system.

This, of course, only egged the audience on even more.

Finally Jazz had stripped down to a tiny black leather bikini.

"What's sexy?" she asked, staring into the camera. "Who knows? My guests today do. Some are real girls. And some are guys who dress like real girls. And they're all hot. But who's hotter? And who cares what people like your third-grade teacher think?"

Here Jazz turned around so that her back was to the audience. Then she undid the top of her leather bikini and pulled it off. She turned her head and spoke over her shoulder.

"The ultimate showdown, real teen girls and transvestite teens. Betcha Mom and Pop don't know what little Bobby wears when he's all alone, know what I mean?"

Jazz smiled a sardonic little smile at the camera. "After all," she concluded, "it's all just *Trash*. Isn't it?"

The show went to a commercial, and Jazz walked off the set, never allowing the audience to see her from the front.

"Pretty amazing, huh?" Barry said, his voice full of admiration.

Many words came to Chelsea's lips, but *amazing* wasn't one of them.

Unbelievable.

Tacky.

Humiliating.

These were but a few of the words that came to Chelsea's lips.

But the valedictorian of Hume-Fogg Honors High School was smart enough to keep her mouth shut.

Because this was *Trash*.

And now she was a part of it.

"Look, how much can we bitch?" Karma asked, carrying her bowl of ice cream into their living room. "I mean, we knew what *Trash* was when we entered the contest to be interns, right?"

It was that evening, and after eating at the Greek diner on the corner, the three girls had come home to find a note on their door from Nick, Sky, and Adam, telling them they'd stop over about nine-thirty.

The girls had changed into shorts, and they had just scooped up three heaping bowls of Ben & Jerry's ice cream they'd bought on the way home.

"Did you apply for a lot of different internships?" Chelsea asked with feigned casualness.

"Just at *Trash* and *The Wall Street Journal*," Karma said, dipping her spoon into her ice cream. "But *Trash* seemed like more fun."

Meaning she got them both, Chelsea realized. *She wasn't rejected three hundred and forty-seven times.*

"*Trash* is the only one I applied for," Lisha said. "A free ticket to New York City, a TV gig, an apartment—I can dig it."

"But doesn't *Trash* seem . . . I don't know . . . even trashier than you thought it would be?" Chelsea asked, spooning some ice cream into her mouth. She thought about her mother's comment about lying down with dogs and getting up with fleas.

It's a good thing she's never watched Trash, Chelsea thought, *or she would drag me home so fast I wouldn't know what hit me.*

"The way I look at it," Lisha said, "is that it's a means to an end. We've all got summer jobs in TV, right?"

"Right," Karma agreed. "So who cares if it's the sleaziest TV ever broadcast in the history of TV? The whole world is sleazy today."

"I guess," Chelsea said reluctantly. She shuddered as she recalled a scene from the show that day: a seventeen-year-old girl in a pushing fight with a tall, thin, desperate-looking transvestite guy who was wearing the same outfit the girl was wearing. "It's just so . . . so sad. And sordid."

"People like sordid," Lisha said. "They like to see weird, dysfunctional people on TV. It makes them feel so superior." She spooned some ice cream into her mouth. "Remember my mom, Chels?"

"Sure," Chelsea said. "She was so sweet. She used to bake the best chocolate-chip cookies. . . ."

"She still does," Lisha said. "And she still teaches Sunday school. But she's addicted to talk shows, the trashier the better."

"Your *mother*?" Chelsea asked in shock.

"Wake up and smell the cappuccino," Karma advised. "These shows are wildly popular. And *Trash* is the most popular of all."

"I guess. . . ." Chelsea said with a sigh.

"People love the titillation," Karma continued. "And then, Jazz has this way of turning the worst of pop culture on its head, you know what I mean? And she's got that in-your-face I-don't-give-a-damn-what-you-think thing, which they love on the college campuses. Face it, it's brilliant."

"But—"

"And just because you work there, it doesn't mean *you're* trash," Lisha added. "Like I said, it's just a gig."

"Yeah . . ." Chelsea agreed reluctantly.

"Hey, you want to be this TV producer right?" Lisha asked. "How do you think Geraldo started?"

"And he's a lawyer, too," Karma put in, licking some ice cream off her spoon.

"Y'all are right, I guess," Chelsea said.

"Someday when Barbara Walters is interviewing you, you'll be able to say how you started out as an intern on the sleaziest show in the history of TV. It'll make a great story."

Chelsea smiled at Lisha. "When we were kids you wanted to be a rock star," she recalled.

"Too bad there aren't any rock-and-roll internships available," Lisha said. She made a face. "God, I was such a joke. Pudgy, buck-toothed little me, a rock star."

"You were cute," Chelsea said loyally. "I mean, you're cuter now . . . how did you do it, anyway?"

"What?" Lisha asked.

"Make yourself over," Chelsea replied.

Lisha shrugged—something she seemed to do whenever she didn't want to answer a question.

"Well, now you're a total babe," Karma said. "So maybe you could tell me how to put on ten pounds of curves—and three inches in height while you're at it."

"You're tiny and darling," Chelsea told her.

"I am so sick of being tiny and darling," Karma whined. "I want to be tall and intimidating, like Roxanne. What's her deal, anyway?"

"I don't know," Lisha said. "I saw her in the hall after the show, and she asked me who I was. Then she just walked away."

"Very bizarre," Karma said. "I get a major bad vibe from her."

"My guess is she's a Jazz wannabe," Lisha said, getting up to put her ice-cream bowl in the sink.

Karma checked her watch. "Oh, wow, I gotta go. My shift starts in an hour."

Chelsea had completely forgotten about Karma's night job as a bartender at Jimi's.

"Aren't you beat?" she asked as Karma raced around gathering up her stuff.

"What can I tell you, I have the energy of an elephant," Karma said. "Remember to triple-lock the door after I leave."

As Karma opened the door Nick, Alan, and Sky practically fell into the apartment.

"What did you do," Sky asked, "just divine that we were out here?"

"I'm on my way to my other job," Karma explained. "And don't bring Belch in unless you gave him a bath since yesterday. I found dog hair on everything."

"She doesn't mean it," Nick told Belch as the three guys and the dog came into the apartment.

"Anybody want ice cream?" Chelsea offered.

"I'm stuffed," Alan said, sitting in the comfortable chair. "We just ate at the Mexican restaurant on Broadway. It was great."

"They wouldn't let Belch in," Nick said, roughhousing with the dog.

"'Cuz—I don't know if this concept has escaped your notice—he's a dog," Lisha pointed out.

"Shhh," Nick said. "Belch doesn't know that."

"I'm beat, man," Sky said, sitting on the rug, right next to Lisha. He lifted a lock of her hair and let it drop. "How about you?"

"I didn't do anything any more strenuous than file papers," Lisha said.

"I answered some guy's phone all day," Alan

said. "It never rang. I don't know who he is or what he does."

"What did you do?" Chelsea asked Nick, trying to sound casual. Just being near him made her feel quivery.

Nick lay down on the rug and Belch climbed on his stomach. "Not much," he said.

"Like what?" Chelsea asked.

"I didn't get there until after lunch," Nick said.

"And no one even noticed?" Lisha asked him.

He put his hand in Belch's mouth, and the dog play-bit at him. "Jazz told me I didn't have to come in until one."

"Jazz?" Lisha repeated. "What, you mean you *know* her?"

"Yeah," Nick said, pushing some hair off his face. "I met her in a club downtown about a month ago. That's how I got this gig."

"I guess that means the contest was fixed," Sky said wryly. "It's an American scandal."

"So, you mean Jazz Stewart, like, walked up to you in a club and said, 'Do you want to be an intern on my show?'" Lisha asked dubiously.

Belch licked Nick's face, and Nick laughed. "Kinda," he replied. "I mean, we talked, and then we went out for coffee, and then she asked me."

"You're kidding, right?" Lisha asked.

"Hey, look at the guy," Alan said in his gentle voice. "I've only known him for two days and I already know that gorgeous women, total

61

strangers, will stop him on the street to give him their phone number."

"It doesn't mean anything," Nick mumbled.

"So, since we're all earning squat, I guess it's my man Nick here who could put in a good word for us about a raise," Sky teased.

"He's probably earning more than we are," Lisha said. She looked over at Nick. "Are you?"

"Hey, chill with that," Nick said, sounding embarrassed. "It's no big thing."

Nick put his hand out and reached for Chelsea, barely making contact with her knee. "You aren't gonna tease me about this, too, are you?"

"Maybe," she said, trying to sound as cool as Lisha always sounded.

What I really want to do is to fling my body on top of you and kiss you wildly, Chelsea thought. *And then I want to—*

"I guess Nick could ask Jazz if he's making more money than we are," Sky said, folding his arms behind his neck.

"Really soon," Alan added, nodding.

"Why, you have her home phone number?" Lisha asked.

"Better," Sky said with a grin. "There was a message on the answering machine when we got in. Jazz is picking Nick up tonight in her limo at eleven o'clock."

Sky leaned into Lisha and nudged her playfully in the shoulder. "But I don't think it's raises that they're gonna talk about, do you?"

There was more teasing banter, but Chelsea didn't hear it. She was too depressed.

Great, she thought. *Just great. I get a crush on a guy, and it turns out he's dating Jazz Stewart, the girl* People *magazine calls the sexiest girl in the world.*

Just great.

O h, no!
Chelsea looked down at the sidewalk, hoping against hope that what she'd just stepped in had been an ice-cream sandwich someone had dropped on the sidewalk by accident, or maybe even a Chinese eggroll that had fallen off some delivery guy's bicycle.

No such luck.

"Yuck," she muttered. "Yuck, yuck, yuck."

Quickly, she pulled on the leashes of the two dogs she was walking, yanking them toward the street, and began scraping her right shoe furiously against the well-worn concrete curb.

Oh yes, she thought to herself, lifting up her foot awkwardly to see if it was now clean. *This is why I left Tennessee. The television business is just soooo glamorous.*

It was a week later, and in that brief span of time Chelsea's mood had gone from euphoria over working in the TV industry, to guilt about the kind of show she was working on, to utter depression at the banal reality of her job.

She spent her days answering phones, filing papers, and doing endless errands for various executives and, most often, for Jazz.

Not that Jazz even knew who she was. Oh, no. It was always Cindy Sumtimes who told Chelsea what Jazz wanted her to do.

Like walking Jazz's two dalmatians, Luke and Ian, which was exactly what she was doing at the moment. Supposedly the dogs were named after two guys from a hit TV show, both of whom Jazz had dated and ditched.

"Come on," Chelsea said impatiently, pulling the two dogs along on their polka-dot leashes. It was only ten o'clock in the morning, and already the air was so hot and humid that her cotton floral dress was sticking to her back.

She'd arrived at the *Trash* studio that morning at nine o'clock, and Cindy Sumtimes had immediately handed her Jazz's dogs, secured by two matching black-and-white polka-dot leashes, and a black-and-white polka-dot cellular phone.

"Don't come back for an hour," Cindy had barked.

"You told me that the last two times I did this job," Chelsea pointed out.

"Yeah, yeah," Cindy said, reaching for a cigarette from the pack in her pocket. "You want Jazz's parasol? It's pretty hot outside."

Chelsea had graciously declined the polka-dot parasol.

I wonder if Jazz wears a polka-dot jumpsuit when she walks these monsters, Chelsea had thought nastily, the dogs pulling on their chains. *Or maybe teenie, tiny polka-dot panties, which she flashes to every cute guy that drives by.*

Luke, the larger of the two dogs, snarled at Chelsea as they turned the corner. "Shut up," she snarled back.

She was in a terrible mood, and Luke and Ian were the very first dogs she had ever met that she could not stand.

"Well, hi, fancy meeting you here," Karma said, coming from the opposite direction on the street. "I see you got the exciting assignment this morning."

Luke snarled again and lifted his leg against a fire hydrant.

"I hate these dogs," Chelsea confessed. "What are you doing out in the real world?"

"Just came from Zabar's," Karma explained. "Had to buy Barry Bassinger his Jamaican coffee beans. You know he doesn't touch the swill we drink in the lounge."

Ian lifted his leg and added his urine to Luke's, barely missing a passerby, who swore as she hurried past.

"I ran into Lisha on Eighty-ninth Street," Karma continued. "She had to pick up Jazz's

67

dry cleaning. Do you think the guys get assigned as much crap work as we do?"

"Alan is doing something or other boring with credit-card receipts," Chelsea reported. "Sky gets to follow a camera guy around all day—lucky him. And Nick never seems to be around at all."

"Oh, he's probably around—around Jazz," Karma said knowingly. She adjusted the suspenders that held up her red raw-silk baggy pants, under which she wore a cropped, sleeveless, purple-and-red-striped shirt.

"It's so gross," Chelsea said crossly. "It's like he's her boy-toy."

"Nice toy if you can get it," Karma said with a grin.

Chelsea made a face at her. "Very funny. You'd just think that Nick would have more self-respect than that, wouldn't you?"

Karma nudged her elbow into Chelsea's side. "You only say that because you're crazed for him."

"I am not!" Chelsea denied vehemently.

"You lie like a rug," Karma said good-naturedly.

"I'm not interested in him," Chelsea insisted, her face turning red.

"You are a terrible liar," Karma said with a grin. "You turn this really bright red color. It's just hilarious!"

Chelsea blushed even harder. "I am not into Nick," she said again. "Anyway, according to

Alan, not only is he spending time with Jazz, but he's had two other girls over this week."

"Gawd, I miss everything by working nights," Karma whined.

"And besides," Chelsea continued, "it just so happens that I like Alan. Really."

"Alan is a doll," Karma agreed. "But Nick turns your bones to jelly."

Luke snarled at Chelsea, and then Ian barked at her.

"I gotta walk these monsters," Chelsea said as the dogs began to pull her away. "I'll see you later."

"Have a blast," Karma called as she headed back toward the *Trash* offices.

Chelsea walked across to West End, where Ian and Luke stopped and sniffed every hydrant, picking their two favorites to stop and deposit their doggie doo. Chelsea dutifully picked it up in the black-and-white plastic bag that Cindy had given her, which she deposited in the nearest street-corner garbage can.

"Hey, pretty mama." A toothless guy on the corner leered at her. Chelsea had already learned to ignore this sort of behavior. She pulled the dogs away from another hydrant, and the black-and-white cellular phone in her pocket rang.

"Chelsea Jennings, intern," she answered.

"How many?" Cindy's voice demanded.

"I'm sorry," Chelsea said, feeling a little weird to be holding a work-related conversation right in the middle of the street, and completely baffled by what Cindy was asking about. "I don't understand."

"Then let me spell it out," Cindy said, exasperated. "How many times did each of Jazz's dogs poop?"

"You're kidding," Chelsea replied, the words popping out of her mouth before she could think about them.

"About Jazz's dogs' poop I don't kid," Cindy replied. "Now, Jazz is sitting right across the table from me, and she really wants to know. She's concerned that Luke and Ian need to go to the vet because of some digestive thing. So you'd better answer me in like two seconds flat. Got it?"

Chelsea nodded, even though Cindy couldn't see her. "Uh, right," she said. "They both went twice, I think."

"You think, or you know?"

"I know," Chelsea answered firmly.

"Gotcha," Cindy said. "Call me when you get back."

My life is so glamorous, Chelsea thought as she tried to lead the dogs back toward the office. They were not interested.

"Come on," Chelsea said impatiently, tugging on their leashes.

Luke trotted over to her.

"Good dog," she told him, reaching down to pat him on the head.

Whereupon he lifted his leg and peed on her

favorite shoes as if they were the nearest fire hydrant.

"Hey, girlie! That dog just—" the toothless guy began, pointing at her shoes.

All Chelsea could do was to turn around and head miserably back for the *Trash* offices, her feet squishing every revolting step of the way.

Chelsea was in the world's most terrible mood. Stopping at a cheap shoe store to replace her ruined shoes had done nothing to improve her mood.

"Hi," Nick said, walking into the employee lounge.

It was two hours later, and Chelsea was on her lunch break. None of her friends had been free, so she had bought a tunafish sandwich at the deli across the street and glumly brought it back to eat in the lounge.

"Hi," Chelsea said, taking a sip of her Coke. "You on lunch?"

"Kinda," Nick said. "I mean, I just got here." He put some coins in the Coke machine and pushed a button.

"Must be nice," Chelsea said, an edge to her voice.

Nick shrugged and popped open his Coke.

"I mean, you never have to do the demeaning things the rest of us do, do you?" she continued. "You never walk dogs, or pick up dry cleaning, or call restaurants you'll never see the inside of to make reservations for other people."

Nick sat next to her on the couch and took a slug of his Coke. "That's what they've got you doing?"

"I haven't used my brain since I got here," Chelsea fumed. "But then again, neither have you."

Nick shook some hair off his face. "You ticked off at me or something?"

"Oh, no," Chelsea said sarcastically, "why would I be ticked off just because you basically slept your way into your job?"

"Who says so?" he asked.

"It's obvious." Chelsea got up and threw the paper from her sandwich into the overflowing trash barrel, then turned to Nick again. "I hope you're not going to tell me you got hired because you wrote a great essay or something like that."

"You think I can't write a great essay?" he asked mildly.

"I don't really care," Chelsea said coolly. "I mean, I don't even know if you graduated from high school."

"Is that important?" Nick asked.

"In your case, evidently not," Chelsea said.

Nick stood up. "Hey, did I do something to you or something? I mean, did you have a dream where I was real wicked to you, and now you're taking it out on me?"

"I don't dream about you!" Chelsea insisted. She could feel her face growing red, since that was a big, fat lie. In fact, she spent most of her nights dreaming about him.

And a lot of her days, too.

"I had a dream about you," Nick said, his voice low. He walked over to Chelsea and stood close enough so that she could hear him breathing.

"You did not," she managed, unable to look him in the eye.

"I did," he said softly. "And you were a lot nicer in the dream."

He picked his Coke up from the table and walked to the door, then turned back to her. "Oh yeah, one other thing. I graduated from high school. A year early. And then I got a scholarship to McGill University." He put his hands in the pockets of his faded jeans. "Later," he added, and walked out the door.

Chelsea sat down on the couch and put her face in her hands. "You are a total idiot!" she yelled out loud. "What did you just do? You wrecked everything!"

Nick stuck his head back into the lounge. "No, you didn't," he said.

Oh my God, he heard me, Chelsea realized, her face burning with embarrassment and humiliation. *Please just let the floor open up and let me fall through it, right now. . . .*

Nick flashed his incredible smile at her. "Don't worry about it. I've been thinking about you, too."

And then he was gone.

"Hi, Cindy?" Chelsea said into the phone in the lounge. "This is Chelsea. I just finished lunch. What did you want me to do?"

"It's not Cindy," the girl replied.

"I'm sorry," Chelsea said quickly. "Did I dial the wrong extension? I was trying to reach—"

"It's Julia," the voice said.

It sure sounded like Cindy.

"Uh . . . Julia?" Chelsea asked carefully.

"I was Cindy last week. This week I prefer Julia," Cindy-Julia said. "Anyway, everyone just calls me Sumtimes. Like sometimes I'm one name and sometimes I'm another. Get it?"

"Right, got it." Chelsea was trying hard not to laugh, since she had a feeling that Cindy-Julia did not find this amusing.

"Okay," Sumtimes said. "Go to Room 401, fourth floor, left out of the elevator. You'll find some of the other interns there, and they'll bring you up to speed. Good luck. You'll need it."

Click.

Chelsea took the stairs rather than wait for the endless elevator, then she made her way through the small warren of offices to Room 401, dodging producers and other staff people who always seemed to be on the run. She pushed open the door to the room.

As Sumtimes had said, there were Alan, Karma, and Lisha, each of them sitting at a separate desk in front of a computer, typing away, with a set of headphones perched on their heads.

They all looked up when Chelsea walked in.

"Hi," Lisha said, slipping off her earphones. "Welcome to insanity."

"What are you doing?" Chelsea asked.

"Listen to this," Alan said, pushing a couple of buttons on the panel in front of his desk. "You're not going to believe it."

The sound of Jazz Stewart's famous voice issued from one of the speakers in the room.

"Hey, this is Jazz," Jazz's voice said coolly. "Thanks for calling 1-900-I'M TRASH! That's right, it's your chance to be with me, Jazz, live on TV, coast-to-coast, and now in Holland and Argentina, too! Just tell me why you should be on my show, and what your TRASHy show idea is. Leave your name and address and phone number, too! This call costs you just a buck ninety-nine a minute. Oh yeah, if you're under eighteen, get the parentals' permission—big duh. Go for it at the beep!"

Alan pushed another button to cut off the recording and shook his head ruefully. "Can you deal? They actually pay for the privilege of leaving Jazz a message."

"It's kind of fiscally brilliant," Karma commented, "when you think about it. A thousand calls a day, more or less, at two bucks, and that's if they talk fast. I bet they make a million a year."

"And I'll bet it's people who can least afford it who make calls to her," Alan said sadly. "It doesn't seem right."

"No one's making these people call," Lisha said with a shrug.

Chelsea edged over to the empty desk and chair next to Alan and sat down. Obviously, it was meant for her, as there was a blank computer screen and keyboard and a set of headphones. And obviously, her friends were transcribing the calls, presumably so that the producers could see if any of them were worth using as a show idea.

"So, what kind of stuff do people suggest?" Chelsea asked.

Alan grinned. "Listen and weep," he said. He pushed another couple of buttons on his panel. Instantly, a girlish voice with a flat Midwest accent filled the room.

"Oh, yeah, hi, Jazz, um . . . my name is Margie Blackwell, and I think you should do a show on sexy mothers and their sexy teen daughters. And it should be, like, a competition, you know? Where the mothers and daughters go out and try to pick up guys, and whoever picks up the cutest guy wins? And, like, you, Jazz, would be the judge. My mother and I volunteer because we do this together all the time here in—"

Alan snapped off the sound and looked at Chelsea, whose jaw was hanging slack with shock.

"You're kidding me," she said.

"No kidding," Lisha commented. "It must be a trend out there in the heartland, 'cause I had some girl in Nevada suggest the same thing on my tape."

Chelsea tried to picture her own mother in a sexy outfit. The idea was so ludicrous that she almost laughed out loud.

"We better get cracking," Karma said. "If Sumtimes catches us talking, she'll probably grow hair."

Chelsea put her headset on. She turned on the computer, which automatically booted to a screen entitled 1-900 SHOW IDEAS, with the day's date on it. Chelsea pushed a switch on the control panel that read PLAY, and the voice of a teen guy filled her headphones.

"Hi, Jazz!" the voice said. "I'm calling from Bend, Oregon. Wow, I can't believe I'm talking to you. Wow, this is so awesome. So, listen, I totally love you. I mean for real. Like, I would marry you, no lie. Call me sometime, but not too late because my parents are like prison guards. Here's my number and you can call collect if you have to. . . ."

Chelsea shook her head in disbelief.

He called to propose marriage to Jazz, and paid two dollars for the privilege? Who would do anything that stupid? she thought.

Do I enter it as a show idea? Probably not. I guess I'll just type his name and number and type Marriage Proposal *next to it.*

For the next half hour Chelsea listened to, and carefully transcribed, many show ideas.

There was the two teen girls in New Hampshire who wanted to have a beer-guzzling contest on the air.

There was the guy in Arkansas who claimed to have slept with four of his high-school teachers. And he was still in high school.

There was a girl in Florida who claimed that she knew at least four other girls who, like her, were really space aliens.

Yeah, right. Chelsea chuckled to herself as she dutifully typed in the call.

And then, there was a call that stopped her heart.

"Yeah," a gravelly young male voice said, as if he'd been chain-smoking for years. "My name is Wade Cooley. My dad's in prison doing time for murder, and my mom's in prison doing time for murder. What a family, huh? It would be bitchin' if you did a show on teens whose parents are murderers, you know? Like, you'd never believe how normal I look. Hey, you guys pay for hotels and stuff, right? So, here's my phone number. . . ."

Chelsea snapped off the tape player. Her hands were trembling and she felt sick to her stomach.

Because from a sicko *Trash* point of view, Chelsea knew this was a terrific show idea, exactly the kind of thing that Jazz loved to do.

I could ignore the tape, Chelsea thought, her

hands growing clammy, her heart pounding in her chest. *No one will ever know that this guy called in.*

But what if Sumtimes comes and checks my work? What if she listens to the tape and finds that I skipped a message? What if, what if, what if . . .

No way out.

Slowly, shakily, she started to type in the information from the tape.

She felt a tap on her shoulder, and jumped guiltily into the air.

"What's your problem?" Roxanne Renault asked, staring down at her.

Chelsea took off her headphones. "You startled me."

"Like a rabbit?" Roxanne asked, looking her over. "Yeah, you kind of have rabbit coloring."

Chelsea's friends kept typing, watching her out of the corners of their eyes.

"Did you want something?" Chelsea asked, trying to sound polite.

Roxanne shook her gorgeous red hair out of her eyes. "You're Chutney, right?" she asked.

"Chelsea. And you're Roxi—"

"Roxanne," the tall girl corrected her. "Only my friends call me Roxi."

Chelsea was taken aback by the girl's utter nastiness. She really didn't know what to say.

"So, how's it going?" Roxanne asked, though she sounded utterly bored.

"Fine," Chelsea said. "We're all . . . you know . . .

um, transcribing the phone calls to the nine-hundred number." She hated the way she sounded—tentative and stupid.

"Anything hot?" Roxanne asked.

"Uh . . ." Chelsea's heart hammered in her chest.

"It wasn't such a tough question," Roxanne said.

"Well, no, I don't think so," Chelsea lied. Sweat began to trickle down the center of her back.

"It doesn't sound as if you'd know something hot if it jumped up and bit you," Roxanne said with disgust. "When you're done, print it all out and bring it to my office.

"If there's anything hot on there," she finished smugly, "I'll find it."

"So," Barry said to Chelsea as the waiter brought over their drinks—Glenlivet single-malt Scotch on the rocks for him, cranberry juice for her. "Here's to a great summer for the one and only Chelsea Jennings!"

He picked up his glass and held it above the bar, for a toast. Chelsea took her cranberry-juice glass self-consciously and clinked it lightly against Barry's.

"Here's to a great summer," she echoed, hoping that her voice didn't betray her nervousness.

She looked around the bar of the Empire Hotel, right across from Lincoln Center. Everywhere she looked, beautiful, sophisticated-looking people were drinking, laughing, talking about their sophisticated lives, she supposed.

"I'm glad you decided to have a drink with me," Barry said with a smile. "When I saw you in the employee lounge this afternoon, you were kinda long in the tooth, as we say. You looked like you needed a friend."

Chelsea stared into her cranberry juice. "I guess . . . I was kind of having a bad day," she admitted.

"Feeling better now?"

"Much," Chelsea said, and she found, to her surprise, that she actually was.

I mean, so what if Luke ruined my favorite shoes, and so what if I spent my day doing stupid errands and typing out crazy ideas from the 900 line. And so what if Roxanne seems to hate my guts for absolutely no reason, and I made a total jerk out of myself in front of Nick.

Here I am, out for drinks with Barry Bassinger, senior producer. He's nice and friendly and he seems to be on my side.

"It was nice of you to invite me," she added.

"Hey, I know how tough it can be," Barry said, swiveling around on the bar stool to face her. "A new town, new job, new faces—I've been there."

He took a sip of his drink and Chelsea studied him. Though small, he was good-looking, and he dressed like a teenager. Today he was wearing jeans, sneakers, and an old Ozzy Osbourne T-shirt, underneath a great-looking black sport jacket with padded shoulders and a slim, European cut.

And everyone seemed to know him, from the coatcheck girl to the bartender. In fact, they were practically fawning over him.

I guess it helps to be a senior producer on the

hottest TV show on the air, Chelsea thought as a beautiful woman stopped to chat with Barry.

"Sorry," he said, after the woman left. "Didn't mean to ignore you."

He's so kind, Chelsea realized, her heart warming. *I guess there really is one nice person who works at* Trash—*besides the interns.*

He took a sip of his drink and studied her. "So, what do you think of *Trash* so far?"

"It's really great!" Chelsea replied brightly.

He raised his eyebrows at her, an amused look on his face.

"I mean, I'm so lucky to be an intern. . . ." Her words sounded lame and hollow even to her own ears.

"A real dream come true, huh?" Barry said, his face still amused.

"Right!" Chelsea agreed, her voice too bright.

Barry took a sip of his Scotch. "You know, Chelsea," he said, leaning toward her confidentially, "I was the one who really pushed to get you on the show."

Chelsea was surprised. "You did?"

"I did," he said cheerfully. "Roxi was completely against you—don't ever tell her I told you so. I mean, I'm speaking in total confidence here, and—"

Another gorgeous woman stopped to talk with him.

Chelsea rubbed her finger nervously along the rim of her glass. Roxi. Roxanne Renault. Just the sound of her name filled Chelsea with dread.

Tomorrow Roxanne would be reading through the show ideas Chelsea had transcribed.

Which means tomorrow she could decide that teen children of murderers is a great topic for a show, she thought, her stomach turning over. *Which means—*

"Sorry," Barry said, turning back to her. "Where was I? Oh, yeah. A group of us went through the finalists. We had it narrowed down to eight, and we were only going to take six. We had to drop one girl and one guy. . . ."

Chelsea nodded again.

"So Karma and Lisha were in. I mean, Karma is so cool she could be a *Trash* covergirl, right? What with her making all that money in the stock market—"

"She what?" Chelsea interrupted.

"She didn't tell you about that?" Barry asked. "The girl is brilliant. She's been dabbling in the stock market for two years. She's made thousands. Her record is better than some of the top analysts—it just slayed us! And she said on her application that her goal was to be a millionaire by the time she's thirty, and to own a TV station before she's forty. Cool, huh?"

"Wow." Chelsea marveled. "I thought she was just into designer fashions. . . ."

"It doesn't hurt that she's Asian and gorgeous, either," Barry admitted. "And Lisha . . . well, after spending a year bumming around Europe—"

"Lisha spent a year in Europe?" Chelsea echoed.

"You didn't know?" Barry asked. "What, don't you guys talk to each other?"

"We do," Chelsea said. "At least, I thought we did."

"Well, anyway, she's utterly cool, smart, confident, hot looking—and ask her about Europe," he added. "So it came down to you and a girl from Alaska who's a sled dogger."

Chelsea felt overwhelmed, and suddenly very depressed. She looked down at her little dress and the cheap shoes she'd run out to buy to replace her wrecked ones.

I'm ordinary, she thought. *I'm utterly ordinary. And the only thing that makes me anything but ordinary is a big, horrible, shameful secret that I can never, ever share with anyone. . . .*

"Hey, I didn't tell you all this to bum you out!" Barry reached out to chuck her lightly under the chin. "I wanted you to know how special I thought you are—how special I still think you are!"

Chelsea tried to smile. "The truth of the matter is . . . well, ever since I got the letter telling me that I got this internship, I've been trying to figure out why I was picked," she confessed. "There are a million girls out there like me—"

"Exactly!" Barry exclaimed.

"Pardon me?" she asked, confused.

"Roxi said you were boring and preppie. She passed your photo around with your two front

85

teeth blacked out with a Magic Marker—I guess she did that herself—and the word *hick* written in real big letters."

Chelsea felt as if someone had punched her in the stomach. "But . . . but that's so mean—"

"I said, 'Rox, there are a million girls out there like Chelsea—smart, cute, all-American-type girls in the hinterlands. What we need around here is that real Middle America thing. It'll be refreshing—someone who isn't jaded and experienced!'"

"I guess that means my essay didn't fool you," Chelsea said.

"You mean where you pretended to be a runaway hooker living on the street?" Barry laughed. "No runaway hooker has the vocabulary you used. It was priceless!"

Chelsea's face burned with embarrassment. "Meaning that you were all laughing at me."

"Hey, don't feel bad," Barry said, reaching out to touch her arm. "We picked you as an intern, didn't we?"

"You did," she agreed.

"Right," he said cheerfully. "As far as I'm concerned, at *Trash*, you are a breath of fresh air. I pushed for you big time, and here you are."

"I guess you have more power than Roxanne," Chelsea said.

"She started last summer as an intern," Barry confided. "She thinks she's hot stuff because she hangs out with Jazz. I mean, give me a break. She's, like, nineteen years old and she grew up

86

in Seattle! What's so exciting about that? I'd better have more power than her, huh?"

"She hates me," Chelsea admitted. "Now I know why."

"Oh, don't mind Roxi," Barry said. "She comes on like she's so tough—she'll chill out after a while."

"Well, it's really nice of you to tell me all this," Chelsea said.

Barry smiled at her. "Like I said, Chelsea, I'm on your side. What can I tell you? I have a weakness for cute, smart, preppie girls."

Chelsea tried to smile back, but her mouth felt funny.

Is he flirting with me? she wondered nervously. *Nah, he couldn't be. He has to be at least thirty-five years old! And* Trash *is filled with gorgeous women. No, he's just being nice.*

"The way I figure it," Barry went on, "so much of our audience is in places like Nashville, and Little Rock, and Oklahoma City, that we need interns and fresh blood from places like that. Do you know there hasn't been a single week since we went on the air when our Nielsens haven't gone up in Coeur d'Alene, Idaho?"

"No, I didn't know that," Chelsea said honestly, remembering dimly from someplace that the Nielsens were the important television ratings, and that talk shows like *Trash* lived and died on their results.

"Everyone says we have to concentrate on sweeps," Barry continued, taking a big slug of his Scotch. "But I think that if we don't do the week-to-week thing well, we're in big trouble. What do you think?"

What do I think? Chelsea thought. *I barely know what he's talking about.*

"I, uh, agree with you, Barry," she stammered.

"I guessed you would." He smiled broadly. "So, tell me what you think."

"About what?" Chelsea asked, picking up a shelled almond from a bowl on the bar and nibbling it nervously.

"About *Trash*, of course," Barry said. "You must be thinking about the show. Hell, I think about it all the time. Give me the interns' perspective. Hell, tell me your best show idea. Here's your chance. Better yet, why don't you give it to me over dinner? They make a great steak here."

"Oh, that's really nice of you." Chelsea glanced quickly at her watch. She had been stuck transcribing tapes until seven, and it was already eight-thirty. "But I'm meeting my friends down at Jimi's at nine-thirty. That's where—"

"Karma's night gig," Barry put in. "I know. It was on her application. Okay, so you're booked." He sounded slightly annoyed and reached for a handful of almonds. "Anyway, that's cool." He looked deeply into Chelsea's eyes. "I want you to know you can talk to me, Chelsea. Really talk to me."

"Thanks."

He chewed the almonds contemplatively. "I

88

bet you're getting sick of the scut work they've got you doing, am I right?"

"Kind of," Chelsea admitted.

"Of course you are," Barry said. "I know how smart you are. And I'll bet you have all kinds of creative ideas, and there you are, you're walking Jazz's monsters—"

Chelsea laughed. "You call them that, too?"

"I hate 'em," Barry said with a laugh. He leaned toward her. "So, Chelsea, listen. I'm not like that. I value your brains. You got a show idea? I want to hear it."

Chelsea's heart nearly skipped a beat. Was the senior producer of *Trash*, the person on whom Jazz leaned more than anyone else, actually asking her for her ideas for a perfect *Trash* show?

What an opportunity, she thought.

Don't blow this, Chelsea.

"You want to hear my best show idea," she said, buying some time.

"That's what I said," Barry said, looking soulfully into her eyes.

Chelsea did have a show idea. And she was convinced that it was a good one. She'd just been waiting for the right chance to tell someone about it, but she was also convinced that no one would listen to her because she was just an intern.

"Here's my idea," she said, choosing her words carefully. "I think that *Trash* should introduce a bunch of teens from all over America to each other by computer, on the Internet, and

89

then bring them on the show and see if they really like each other. If they do, great. If they don't, it's TRASH!"

There. She'd done it. She had agonized over this idea many nights in the dark, before she'd gone to sleep, and had finally decided that it conformed both with her personal value system and with the kind of shows that Jazz tended to do.

It's actually moral, Chelsea thought, *something I could feel proud of. It doesn't exploit anyone. And if it works, it would show everyone that* Trash *doesn't have to be so sleazy to be successful. . . .*

She waited, holding her breath. Barry stared intently into her eyes.

"Brilliant," he finally said. "It's so . . . brilliant."

"It is?" Chelsea asked, shocked.

"Totally," he affirmed. "I knew I was right when I picked you, Chelsea. You've got a creative mind—"

"My honors English teacher told me the same thing!" she said with excitement.

"Chelsea Jennings, you are definitely going places," Barry predicted with a smile. He picked up his drink and drained it.

"I can get your idea on the air," he said. "Listen, what say we go over to my apartment? I know you can't drink here because they've got that stupid underage law, but I've got plenty of Glenlivet at my place. We can talk about your idea and whatnot."

"B-but I have to meet my friends downtown," Chelsea stammered.

"Oh, yeah, right," Barry said. He put his hand on her arm and rubbed softly. "But this could be much more important. *Much*," he added significantly.

"Oh, gosh, I couldn't stand them up," Chelsea heard herself say.

I sound like a ten-year-old, she thought. *A really stupid ten-year-old. And I'll bet he was only pretending to like my idea so I'd go back to his apartment with him. And now that I turned him down he's going to be really mean—*

"Hey, no prob," Barry said, dropping some money on the bar. He stood up. "So, did I cheer you up just a little?"

Chelsea stood up, too, and happiness flooded through her. So he wasn't a jerk! He really was a good guy! Impetuously she leaned over and planted a kiss on his cheek. "You cheered me up a lot," she said. "Thank you."

"Don't mention it," Barry said easily. "I'll be thinking a lot about your great show idea. Let me help you get a cab downtown, okay?"

Barry gave her a quick hug before he put her into the taxi, which he insisted on paying for, and Chelsea sat back as the driver zoomed wildly in and out of Manhattan traffic.

Well, well, well, she thought. *So Barry Bassinger really is a good guy after all. He likes my idea. And he likes me.*

And he has a lot more power than Roxanne.

*   *   *

"ID," a three-hundred-pound bouncer in a black leather jacket said, holding his hand out.

"I thought you didn't have to be twenty-one here—"

"You gotta be *under* twenty-six," the bouncer explained, still holding his hand out.

"Oh, that's right, I forgot." Chelsea scrambled in her purse for her driver's license and flashed it at the bouncer.

"Tennessee?" he said. "Is that in America?"

"Very funny," Chelsea said. "You should do stand-up."

"I do," the guy said seriously. "Check me out at the Comedy Factory on Monday nights." He put out a huge, meaty hand. "Five-dollar cover, sweetheart."

Chelsea pulled the one and only five-dollar bill she had out of her wallet and handed it to him. He waved her in.

Outside, Jimi's looked like any gray stone building in New York's so-hip East Village. In fact, there was only the tiniest sign on a blacked-out window that read JIMI'S.

Inside, it was insane.

Loud rock music pulsed off the walls. A large dance floor was lit here and there by colored lights, and on a raised stage area fake snow was falling on the dancers. Against one wall was a bar, but it was too far away and too dimly lit for Chelsea to see if her friends were there.

She looked up. A balcony ran all the way

around the room. She could dimly make out a pool table, and a huge robot-looking mechanical creature wearing a T-shirt that read JIMI.

As the music changed, so did the light, and on the raised area where it had been snowing before, it now rained. Real rain, from some system in the ceiling. The water fell on the dancers, and then disappeared down tiny, recessed drains in the floor.

"Chelsea!" Alan yelled over the pounding music.

"Oh, hi!" she yelled back. "Wow, this place is wild!"

"No kidding! Come on."

Alan took her hand and led her through the maze of bodies until they reached the bar in the corner.

"You found us!" Karma said happily from behind the bar. She was wearing a black T-shirt that said JIMI's in bright pink letters. "Want the house special?"

"What is it?" Chelsea asked.

Karma didn't reply; she just poured something orange into a tall glass.

Chelsea took a sip. It was cold and fruity. "This is great!"

"Twelve different fruit extracts," Karma said. "And ginseng, which is supposed to rev up your energy or something like that. My parents live on the stuff."

"Where's everyone?" Chelsea asked, sipping her drink.

"Sky and Lisha are out there dancing somewhere," Alan said.

"Where's Nick?" Chelsea asked, trying to sound casual. It was difficult. Very difficult.

"Nick hasn't shown up yet," Alan said.

"Probably tooling around Manhattan in Jazz's white limo with the polka-dot doors," Karma said. She hurried off to wait on some people farther down the bar.

The music changed to a ballad by Hootie and the Blowfish. Alan smiled at Chelsea. "Dance?"

"Sure," she said.

They walked over to the dance floor—fortunately, it had stopped raining—and Alan took her into his arms. He felt good—warm, comfortable.

"You smell nice," he said, sniffing her hair.

"I doubt it," Chelsea said with a laugh. "I'm still wearing what I wore to work. I never made it home to shower and change."

"You look perfect to me," Alan said softly. "'Shall I compare thee to a summer's day'?" he quoted lightly.

"Shakespeare, right?" Chelsea asked.

"Big Bill himself," Alan confirmed. "Can you imagine one guy writing all that great stuff? It blows me away."

"Maybe you'll write something that great one day," Chelsea said.

Alan laughed. "I doubt it. Sometimes I feel paralyzed just trying to write a short story. I keep hearing my dad's voice in my head, telling me I'm this big, worthless disappointment. Why don't I go out and do something *manly* instead of sitting in my room trying to write?"

"That's so cruel," Chelsea said. "And unfair."

"My dad lives and breathes football," Alan said. "But I never understood the thrill of big guys banging into each other in the mud. What can I say? I'm his only son and a major disappointment."

"Well, that's his loss." Chelsea leaned her head on Alan's shoulder and closed her eyes, swaying to the music.

"Hey, did I mention what a totally great girl I think you are?" he whispered into her hair.

"No," she whispered back. She felt warm and safe and happy. Barry Bassinger liked her show idea. Alan liked her. And she liked Alan.

And he's so much nicer than Nick, she thought. *He's kinder. And more sensitive. And I don't feel like a stuttering idiot around him.*

Slowly Chelsea turned her mouth to Alan's, and she kissed him softly, just at the corner where his lips met his cheek.

"Chelsea," he whispered. His arms tightened around her and he kissed her fully, his body pressed against hers. She kissed him back, wrapping her arms around his neck.

"Yo, the music stopped, you two," Sky said as he walked by, hand in hand with Lisha.

Chelsea opened her eyes. The music really had stopped.

"Hey, I kiss her, I hear music," Alan said lightly, draping his arm around Chelsea's shoulder.

"Having fun?" Lisha asked Chelsea as the music started up again. Kurt Cobain's voice wailed through the sound system.

"It's great here," Chelsea said. Her stomach growled. "Hey, have you guys eaten dinner?"

"No," Lisha said. "I'm starving. Do they serve food here?"

"Karma says it sucks," Sky said. "There's a Thai place down the street we could check out."

"Thai food?" Chelsea asked.

"You've never had it?" Alan said.

She shook her head no. "Believe me, Nashville is a fried-chicken-and-ribs kind of town."

"Well, allow me to broaden your culinary horizons," Alan said.

They went back over to the bar to tell Karma where they were going, then the four of them headed out the door. Alan had his arm draped around Chelsea's shoulders, and Sky was telling a joke that a cameraman at *Trash* had told him that afternoon.

Chelsea looked up, feeling happier than she had felt since she arrived in New York.

There was a white limo parking at the curb. With the famous dalmatian polka dots on the doors.

And there was Nick, getting out of the limo.

And Jazz, jumping into his arms.

"Wonderful girl that I am, I have brought you slackers breakfast," Karma said as she sailed into the apartment the next morning.

It was Saturday, and Chelsea and Lisha were sitting around in T-shirts and cutoffs, drinking coffee and trying to wake up.

After running into Nick and Jazz the night before, Chelsea vowed to herself that she was going to stop wasting her time dreaming about Nick Shaw.

I mean, what more proof do you need? she asked herself. *There was Jazz herself, in Nick's arms.*

At least Nick looked embarrassed, she recalled, taking another sip of her coffee. *And when Alan invited him and Jazz to come to dinner with us, he looked like he wanted to say yes.*

Of course, Jazz wouldn't be caught dead with us. And she just laughed and said they were heading to some chic restaurant down the block. So maybe it was just my imagination that Nick wanted to be with us. . . .

Wanted to be with me.

Yeah, right. What a joke.

After eating at the Thai restaurant—Chelsea was crazy about the coconut soup and the curried chicken—they had gone back to Jimi's, where the four of them had danced until two in the morning.

Alan had kissed her many more times, Chelsea recalled. And it was . . . nice. Not thrilling. Not earth-shattering. But really nice.

Nick's kisses wouldn't be nice, Chelsea thought. *They would sear my lips. They would make me melt. . . .*

"I hope you brought something with lots of sugar," Lisha said in her throaty voice. "I need the rush to wake up."

"Oh, forget sugar, darling," Karma said, setting her bag of groceries on the kitchen table. "We are talking bagels, lox, and cream cheese, better known as Jewish soul food."

"What's lox?" Chelsea asked, padding over to peer into the large brown bag from Zabar's.

Karma stared at her. "Surely you jest." She pulled a copy of *Barron's* out of the bag and set it on the counter.

"I've had bagels," Chelsea said defensively.

"Well, my dear, you have not lived until

you've had a really fresh New York bagel with cream cheese and lox, also known as smoked salmon."

"Smoked, as in . . . raw?" Chelsea asked tentatively.

"It's great," Lisha said, reaching for a packet of oily-looking white paper. "I had it at my exboyfriend's house." She unwrapped the paper. Pale, reddish, fishy-looking things lay there.

"That's it?" Chelsea asked, peering at it dubiously.

"Trust me," Karma said. She took out a poppy-seed bagel, sliced it, and spread it thickly with cream cheese. Then she took some paper-thin slices of the orange fish and put them on top. Then she handed it to Chelsea. "Bite."

Chelsea took the bagel and took a tentative bite. She let the taste swarm around her tongue for a moment. "It's . . . good!" she said with surprise. She took another big bite. "It's fantastic!"

Karma laughed. "She's hooked now. Watch out, world!" She and Lisha quickly made their own bagels, which they carried into the living room, along with fresh cups of hot, strong coffee.

"I love this!" Chelsea said, licking some cream cheese off her finger.

"Good, then we can still be friends," Karma said sweetly. "So, did you guys have fun last night?"

"The Thai food was great," Chelsea said, taking a sip of coffee.

"I wasn't referring to the food," Karma said slyly. "I saw you and Alan sucking serious face on the dance floor."

"He's sweet," Chelsea said.

"I hate sweet," Lisha said blithely.

"What's wrong with sweet?" Chelsea asked.

Lisha sighed. "I don't know. Sweet is just so . . . so *good*. I like bad boys. Well, I used to, anyway."

"My shrink told me that is a very dangerous romantic outlook," Karma said. "Here's his theory. If a girl doesn't like herself, then she thinks she isn't worth anything. Hence, any guy who would like her and treat her well isn't worth anything, either. But if a guy treats her like crap, he's sexy and wonderful." She took a bite of her bagel.

"You're in therapy?" Chelsea asked.

"Not anymore," Karma said. "My parents made me go my junior year of high school. They thought I was antisocial because I stayed in my room reading *Business Week*."

Chelsea remembered what Barry had told her the evening before. "Hey, Barry told me you play the stock market."

"Oh, yeah," Karma said, "here and there."

"I don't even understand how the stock market works," Lisha admitted.

"Me, neither," Chelsea said. She looked over

at Karma. "Barry said you're really good, that you've made a lot of money at it."

"And since when did you and the senior producer get so chummy?" Karma asked.

Chelsea smiled. "He took me out for a drink after work yesterday."

"Get out of here!" Karma cried.

"How soon was it before he tried to put his hand down your dress?" Lisha asked dryly.

"It wasn't like that," Chelsea insisted. "He was just really nice to me."

"Please," Lisha said. "He wants to get in your pants."

"We're just friends," Chelsea said. "He told me a lot of stuff—like why Roxanne hates my guts, for example." She quickly told them what Barry had told her about Roxanne's opposition to Chelsea during the intern selections.

"So, it's just a stupid power struggle?" Karma asked. "And she hates you for that, even though you didn't have anything to do with it?"

"I guess so," Chelsea said.

"She was such a bitch to you yesterday in the computer room," Lisha said. "I wanted to throw my headphones at her."

"I know," Chelsea agreed. "And listen to this! She's only nineteen, and she started at *Trash* as an intern!"

"So, who'd she do to get promoted from intern to . . . whatever it is her job title is—I can't figure it out," Karma said, polishing off her bagel.

101

"Who'd she 'do'?" Chelsea echoed. "What does that mean?"

"It means who'd she have sex with," Lisha translated.

"Oh," Chelsea said, chagrined. "I don't know. Maybe she's just smart and good at her job."

"She's the Wicked Witch of the West, even if she does look like a taller, younger Sharon Stone with better hair," Karma said. "Have you noticed that I come up to, like, her kneecaps?"

Lisha's eyes narrowed. "She's power hungry, if you ask me."

"But what a wardrobe," Karma said with a sigh. "I could kill for that little number she had on yesterday. Of course, the right sleeve alone would've covered my entire body. . . ."

"She's perfect looking." Chelsea sighed, too. "And she knows it."

"Not perfect," Karma said. She rose to get another bagel. "I have found her fatal flaw."

"What?" Lisha asked.

"The dawgs," Karma said, reaching into the bagel bag.

"The what?" Chelsea asked.

"Dawgs—feet," Karma translated. "The girl has feet the size of an ocean liner. She must go a size twelve at least."

"Bigfoot!" Lisha cried with delight. "Now the story can be told—we have found Bigfoot, and she's at *Trash!*"

The girls cracked up.

"Hey, I think there's a *Trash* episode in it!"

Chelsea said. "Teens Who Have Been Stomped by Bigfoot!"

"You could go on the air and tell your sad and tawdry tale," Karma snorted gleefully.

"My guess is that Bigfoot is doing Barry Bassinger," Lisha said, sipping her coffee. "That's how she got her big promotion."

"Oh, no, I don't think so." Chelsea was quick to disagree, loyal to her new friend and mentor, Barry.

"You're being naive," Lisha said. "Barry's the guy with the most power at *Trash*."

"But he's not like that, I mean it," Chelsea insisted.

There was a knock on their door. Karma opened it.

"Notice how she doesn't think it's a mass murderer anymore," Lisha told Chelsea with a laugh.

A mass murderer, Chelsea thought. *Like my father. And Roxanne is going to love the show idea, Teen Kids of Murderers. And everyone is going to find out.*

"Hi," Sky said, leaning on the door frame. "Can a neighbor borrow some coffee?"

"Don't you guys ever shop?" Karma asked as she went into the kitchen for some coffee beans.

"Hi." Sky looked over at Lisha. "How you doing?"

"Fine," Lisha said coolly.

"It's really nice out," he told her. "Want to go to Central Park with me later? We could go for a run, go to the zoo—"

103

"I don't think so," Lisha said. "Thanks anyway."

"Oh, okay," Sky said. Karma handed him the coffee beans. "Well, see you guys later. Hang loose."

Karma shut the door. "Oo, you just broke his heart," she chided Lisha.

"I thought you liked him," Chelsea added.

"I do like him," Lisha said. "I like him the same way you like Alan."

"I'd go to the park with Alan," Chelsea said. "I like Alan a lot."

"What happened to you and Nick?" Karma asked from the kitchen.

"There is no me and Nick," Chelsea said. "That is totally obvious. I'm with Alan. He's with Jazz. End of story."

"Oh yeah, right," Karma snorted, clearly not believing Chelsea.

"I'm serious," Chelsea insisted. "I'm not like you guys. I don't let myself get carried away by a purely physical attraction. I mean, a relationship has to be based on more than that. . . ."

"Well, I don't want any kind of a relationship," Lisha said lightly, getting up from the floor. She put her coffee cup in the sink. "Frankly, I've had it with guys. They're highly overrated."

"Did you get burned or something?" Karma asked, coming back into the living room with her second bagel.

"I just know what can happen when you get in too deep," Lisha said.

"In Europe," Chelsea blurted out.

Lisha and Karma stared at her.

"Something happened to you in Europe—"

"How do you know about that?" Lisha asked sharply.

"I don't," Chelsea confessed. "But Barry said I should ask you about Europe—"

"And Barry should keep his mouth shut." Lisha's voice was tight.

"When were you there, you lucky dog, you?" Karma asked.

"Last year," Lisha said. She sounded closed off and suddenly cold.

"So you were, like, an exchange student?" Karma asked, taking a huge bite of her bagel.

"Something like that," Lisha said. "Hey, how is it that you can eat like that and stay so tiny?" she asked Karma, clearly anxious to change the subject.

Karma went into a long story about her unbelievably fast metabolism. Chelsea thought about what Lisha had just said.

I feel like I don't even know her anymore, Chelsea realized. *It's as if she has these huge secrets and she doesn't really want to let us in. And Karma has made all this money in the stock market, but she acts like she's an airhead. So I guess she has some kind of a secret, too.*

And I have the hugest secret of all, she realized. *And whatever it is that Karma and Lisha are trying to hide, I bet anything that my secret is a hundred times more shocking than theirs.*

"You sure you don't want to come to Jimi's with me?" Karma asked as she buttoned her clear plastic raincoat over her all-black outfit.

A streak of lightning was followed by a deep roll of thunder and wind lashed against their windows. The beautiful day had turned into a stormy night.

"Nah," Chelsea said. "It's so horrible outside. I'm just going to curl up with a book. I don't think I've read anything decent since I got to New York."

"No one reads in New York," Karma teased. "They just read the coverage."

Chelsea laughed. She knew that Karma meant the short descriptions the underlings wrote about possible "properties"—meaning novels, plays, or screenplays—for their bosses, who were too busy to read anything. In fact, Sumtimes had asked Alan to write "coverage" for a new horror novel that supposedly had inspired a teen reader to murder his best friend.

"See how much you've learned here in Sin City?" Karma quipped, reaching into the front closet for an umbrella. She turned back to Chelsea. "You really don't mind staying home alone on a Saturday night?"

Chelsea shook her head no. Lisha had gone to the movies with Sky—though she insisted to him that they were just "friends"—Alan had gone to visit a relative of his who lived in New Jersey, and as per usual, no one knew Nick's whereabouts.

"Don't open the door to anyone," Karma cautioned her. "You know you can't trust Antoine to screen guests."

"Thanks, Mom," Chelsea said with a laugh.

Karma waved and walked out.

She's so nice, Chelsea thought, locking the door behind Karma. *I totally lucked out, ending up roommates with her and Lisha. I haven't really had a best friend since Lisha moved away,* she realized as she padded back into her bedroom to get the book she wanted to read. *I mean, I had tons of friends, but no one to really confide in.*

Not that I could confide my deepest secret to Lisha or Karma, anyway, she told herself. She sat down on her bed, lost in thought.

What would happen, I wonder, if I told them the truth? If I could just talk to them, just confide in them . . .

Never. They'd be horrified, she decided. *They'd watch me every moment, afraid I was going to gun them down in their sleep. They'd want me to move out, but they'd be too afraid to say anything.*

Chelsea shook off these horrible thoughts and grabbed her book. "Just don't think about it," she told herself. "You're not going to say anything, so you don't have to worry about it."

She lay down on her bed and opened her book, *The Chosen,* by Chaim Potok, which Karma said was her favorite novel of all time.

Chelsea was startled by a knock on the front door. She looked at the clock on her dresser. She had been reading for two hours straight without even realizing it.

She walked into the living room and peered through the peephole in the front door. "Who is it?" she called. She could just make out a blurry male figure.

"Ick."

This had become a joke between them all. She opened the door. There was Nick, looking impossibly perfect in worn jeans, a T-shirt, and a flannel shirt. And he didn't even have Belch with him.

"Where's man's best friend?" Chelsea asked.

"He's getting his beauty sleep," Nick said. "Do I get invited in?"

Chelsea shrugged—she hoped she looked as cool and sophisticated as Lisha did when she shrugged—as if she didn't much care what Nick did one way or the other.

"No one's home?" Nick asked, plopping onto the couch.

"Just me," Chelsea said. She sat in the chair near him, but not too near. "So, you're not out with Jazz tonight, huh?"

"I'm here," Nick said, as if that explained everything.

"What, she didn't summon you?" Chelsea sneered.

"I think you have the wrong idea," Nick said. He jumped up from the couch. "Got beverage?" He already had the refrigerator door open.

"Help yourself," Chelsea said dryly.

"Want anything?" Nick asked.

"No."

He came back into the living room with a Coke. "So, how you doing?"

"I *was* doing fine," Chelsea said pointedly. "I *was* reading."

"So I'm disturbing you, in other words," Nick said.

"You're a very perceptive guy," Chelsea replied.

He shook some hair off his face. "I seem to bring out the worst in you, Chelsea. How come?"

She shrugged again.

"I mean, everyone is always saying how nice you are, sweet, good-natured—"

"But you don't think so," Chelsea said.

"Well, you always seem ticked off at me."

"That would presume I care enough about you to *be* ticked off."

"Don't you?" he asked softly.

She couldn't look at him. She got up and went to the CD player, and put on a Tori Amos CD.

"Hey," he said, his voice low.

He was standing right behind her. She could feel his breath on her neck. She didn't turn around.

109

"Look, Chelsea, I knew you were home alone. That's why I stopped over. I wanted to talk to you."

Still, she didn't turn around.

"You're right," he went on. "I got the gig at *Trash* because Jazz liked me. And yeah, I've been dating her. I thought it would be a kick. I mean, she's beautiful and famous. But I don't care about her. I never, ever cared about her."

Chelsea looked down. She could see her hands trembling. "So why are you dating her, then?" she asked. "Isn't that kind of hypocritical?"

"Yes," Nick said. He reached for her shoulders and gently turned her around. "That's why I'm gonna stop seeing her."

She looked into his blue eyes, eyes as blue as the ocean, eyes she could fall into, fall in love with. . . .

"She'll fire you," Chelsea whispered. "Won't she?"

"I don't know," Nick admitted. "But it's not like I've been doing any work around there, anyway. Jazz just thinks it's a gas to be dating a carpenter—"

"I thought you went to McGill University," Chelsea said.

"I did," Nick said. "But I dropped out. I just couldn't figure out what the hell I was doing there, you know? I mean, what does it all mean, anyway? My dad's a carpenter, and his dad was a carpenter, and they wanted me to go to college so badly."

"And then you dropped out," Chelsea said.

Nick's eyes searched hers. "You can't live anyone's dream but your own. Don't you know that?"

"I . . . I . . ." She felt as if she couldn't get her breath, couldn't speak.

"Chelsea."

The way he said her name made her knees turn to Jell-O.

He reached for her, slowly pulling her close, until she could feel his heart beating against hers. Then he kissed her hair, her cheek, her neck, until she thought she'd just die if he didn't put his lips on hers, and then finally he did . . .

. . . And the room flew away, there was only the sizzling heat of Nick, Nick's arms, Nick's lips, and her own voice, softly calling his name.

R oxanne "Bigfoot" Renault—Chelsea
couldn't look at her or think of her anymore without snickering inside at their
nickname for her—looked up from the pile of
papers in front of her, and then down her nose
at Karma, Lisha, Alan, and Chelsea, who all
sat across the conference-room table from her.

Evidently, Bigfoot had taken the transcripts
of their tapes from the 900 number home with
her over the weekend. When they had all arrived at work that morning, there was a note
from Roxanne telling them to write up any of
the ideas from their tapes that would make
a good show for *Trash*. These ideas were to
be dropped off in Bigfoot's office within the
hour.

Chelsea had agonized over her transcripts.

*I'm not about to point out that Teen Offspring
of Murderers is a great* Trash *idea,* she thought.

She's going to have to come up with that one herself.

Only please, God, let her miss it.

All Chelsea had written up was an idea from a girl in Michigan, whose entire body was tattooed, and who thought Jazz should be tattooed on the air.

Now it was eleven-thirty, and they were all in Roxanne's office, their transcripts and the ideas they had picked in a big pile on Bigfoot's desk.

"Your ideas all suck, Karma," Bigfoot said to Karma, who Chelsea could see was not in the least bit cowed. "You can go."

Then she looked at Lisha.

"These suck, too, so get out of here," she said to Lisha, in the same cold tone of voice.

"And you, too, Alan," she added, not even looking up at Alan to acknowledge his presence.

Silently, Karma, Lisha, and Alan got up out of their chairs, pushed them under the clear glass table, and left the room. Karma rolled her eyes at Roxanne's feet, clad today in gigunda brown suede heels, which matched her perfectly cut brown silk suit, and walked out.

Bigfoot stretched her long legs, enclosed in sheer hose, ending in those astonishingly large feet, under the table. She shuffled a few papers on the desk as Chelsea waited and watched, growing more anxious by the second.

Roxanne picked up the idea Chelsea had

written up. "A girl who's tattooed?" she asked, her tone withering. "That's your idea of a hip show for *Trash?*"

"Well, maybe we could work with it," Chelsea said tentatively.

"It's stupid. It's lame. It sucks," Roxanne said.

"Gee, I guess that means you don't like it." Chelsea was unable to keep the sarcasm out of her voice.

"Have you got a problem?" Bigfoot snapped at her.

"No," Chelsea said with a sigh.

"There were two usable ideas on your tape," Roxanne said, "not that you picked up on that. Although I can't think of any reason that should surprise me, can you?" Bigfoot stared at her.

"I'm assuming that was a rhetorical question," Chelsea said, trying to keep her voice neutral, lest she antagonize Roxanne even more.

"Oh yes." Roxanne sneered. "I forgot, you went to an honors high school. That's why you know big words like *rhetorical.*"

Chelsea fumed, but kept silent.

"Anyway," Roxanne went on, "there are two good ones here. Barry told me to tell you that he wants you to work on the marriage one as a long-term show concept, though I can't imagine why he'd think you'd be the right intern for it."

"The marriage one?" Chelsea asked. She had no idea what Roxanne was talking about.

"We're gonna bring a whole bunch of different guys who want Jazz to marry them on the show, and let them play the Dating Game. The last one standing gets to do a quick change of uni, then we'll do a civil ceremony right then and there. And then Jazz will divorce him. So call that guy in Bend, Oregon, and tell him he's about to be famous."

"B-but that wasn't a show idea!" Chelsea protested. "That guy was for real."

"You've got to learn you can find trash for *Trash* anywhere," Roxanne pontificated, as if she were repeating an axiom she'd used a hundred times before. "Anyway, those are Barry's orders, not mine. I would have given it to Kushner."

Roxanne shuffled some papers on her desk, read something, then looked back at Chelsea. "Then there's this other one," she said slowly. "A good one. A really good one."

No, no, no, Chelsea screamed inside her head. *Please, don't let it be what I think it is—*

"This children-of-murderers thing," Roxanne went on. "Now, this has really good possibilities."

I knew it. I knew it.

"You totally missed it." Bigfoot was again sneering. "I guess you were too busy getting all rah-rah over girls with tattoos."

Chelsea kept silent.

"Of course, it has no possibilities at all, as is,"

Roxanne continued. "Maybe for *Geraldo* or *Ricki Lake*, but not for *Trash*. You know why?"

"It's been done before?" Chelsea ventured hopefully.

"Wrong," Roxanne said. "Because it's too tame for *Trash*. But I have figured out how to make this the *Trash* hit of all time. Want to know how?"

Chelsea got a sickening feeling in her stomach again.

"How?" she squeaked out.

"We make it into a show about the teen kids of *mass murderers*." Roxanne was leaning forward in her chair, visibly gloating. "Now, am I brilliant, or am I brilliant?"

This cannot be happening, Chelsea thought. *This is my worst nightmare come true. There's got to be something I can do, some way out of this. . . .*

"I mean, think about it," Roxanne went on, her eyes shining, "did Charles Manson have kids? Or what about that guy who shot all those people from the bell tower at the University in Texas years ago? It's so hot, it's sizzling!"

"Uh-huh," Chelsea managed. She felt her stomach turning over.

"I'm going to run with this one all by myself," Roxanne decided. She stood up, clearly meaning that Chelsea should stand up, too, which she did.

"I'm going to find the offspring of the worst

mass murderers of all time," Bigfoot promised. "And believe me, I am the girl to do it."

"Chelsea," Barry said happily, giving her a warm embrace, "it's great to see you again."

"It's good to see you, too, Barry," Chelsea said sincerely as she stood up from her bar stool to embrace Barry back.

Barry and Chelsea were once again in the bar of the Empire Hotel. He had stopped by her tiny cubicle in the early afternoon to see how she was doing.

Chelsea had been sitting there, her head in her hands, agonizing over Roxanne's show about the kids of mass murderers.

All day long she hadn't been able to think about anything else. Not even thoughts of Nick could penetrate her wall of fear and anxiety.

"Hey, killer, you okay?" Barry had asked her.

Killer. Funny joke. If he only knew.

"Oh, yeah, just thinking," she had said lamely.

At which point he had invited her out for a drink after work, to talk about her "terrific show idea."

Anything to get my mind off Bigfoot, Chelsea had thought, and gratefully accepted.

"Cranberry juice, right?" Barry said now. "I took the liberty." A glass of cranberry juice sat on the bar in front of Chelsea.

"Thanks," she said, and took a sip of the cool, tart liquid.

"So, lucky girl," Barry said, a big grin on his face, "I've got great news for you, and I do mean great."

"About my show idea?" Chelsea asked, getting excited in spite of herself.

"I got to pitch it to Jazz this morning." Barry leaned forward conspiratorially. "And she loved it! I mean, she *loved* it!"

"Really?" Chelsea asked, thrilled. "That's . . . that's fantastic!"

"And"—he took a momentous pause—"she wants you to run the damn thing!"

"Me?" Chelsea squeaked. "She wants me—?"

"Well"—Barry chuckled—"I sort of gently nudged her in that direction. I merely suggested that the person who came up with the idea should be the person who puts it into motion."

"I can't believe it!" Chelsea cried. "That was so nice of you, really!"

"Hey, I'm a good guy," Barry said. "And like I told you, I have a weakness for cute, preppie girls with just the tiniest trace of a Southern accent." He traced the line of her hand from her thumb to her wrist.

"Well, I really appreciate it," Chelsea said, casually moving her hand away from him. "I won't let you down."

"Good." Barry grinned. "Because the show's airing on Friday."

Friday? Chelsea thought, astonished. *But that's just four days away from today! How can*

I possibly get this together by Friday? I've never even worked on any part of a real Trash *show before. All I know how to do is walk Jazz's monsters and transcribe tapes.*

"Do you really . . . I mean, how am I supposed to . . . I mean . . . Friday is really soon," Chelsea stammered.

Barry laughed deeply, and took his sport jacket off, so that now all he wore with his jeans was a T-shirt featuring John Mellencamp playing at Farm Aid.

"Hey, not to worry," Barry told her. "You won't be working alone. I'm gonna put Karma and Lisha on it with you, and Sumtimes—she does the work of any three people. I'll be in charge, and I promise not to let you get in over your pretty head, okay?"

Chelsea gulped. "Okay," she said shakily, thinking already of the millions of things that would have to be done in order to get her show together in four days.

"I can see I freaked you out with this," Barry said, patting her thigh. "We don't always work this fast. But Jazz hated the show that was set for Friday, so we canned it. You got a lucky break."

He took a sip of his Scotch. "Jazz said to make this a number-one priority. That means open the checkbook wide. Do you know how many people would kill to be guests on *Trash*, get flown first-class to New York and be put up in The Plaza Hotel?"

"Lots, I suppose," Chelsea said.

Barry chuckled. "Babe, I've seen people quit their jobs for less." Just then he glimpsed someone he knew walk in the door of the bar and gave a quick wave. Then he reached in his pocket, took out an envelope, and handed it to Chelsea.

"This'll give you a head start," he said.

Chelsea tore the letter open and scanned it quickly. It was a memo to Barry, from Sumtimes, detailing some research she'd done about an on-line introduction service called Young Love Online. Evidently, the producer had already talked with the service, which specialized in matching teen guys and teen girls by computer, and the company was ready to cut a deal with *Trash*.

"This is fantastic," Chelsea said, quickly reading the memo. Sumtimes had just saved her hours and hours of hard work.

"I've got some other ideas," Barry said, picking up his drink and draining it. "I'd like to invite you over to my place now—we can continue over there. I've got a cold bottle of Aligote in the fridge. French, it's the best."

"Gee, I can't," Chelsea said. "I mean, I'd like to, but I promised Karma and Lisha we'd see the new Woody Allen movie tonight."

"I just handed you a gig that half the staff would kill for," Barry said sharply.

"I know, and I'm really grateful—"

"You don't act really grateful," Barry told her.

"Well, I want to . . . log on to Young Love Online myself tonight," she said quickly. "I mean, I don't have much time to get this show together. . . ." she improvised.

"A go-getter, huh?" Barry laughed. He threw his hands up in the air. "Okay, I can't argue with that. But I've got a computer at my place. We can log on together. For research." He leaned forward and lifted a lock of Chelsea's hair. "I truly am partial to blondes," he said, his voice low.

"Gosh, look at the time!" Chelsea said, jumping up from the bar stool. "I promised my friends. But I'm sure we'll be working together a lot in the next few days."

Barry grinned. He didn't seem too upset, she realized with relief. "Okay, Chelsea," he said, wagging a finger at her. "We've got plenty of time, right?"

"Right," Chelsea agreed, but she wasn't exactly sure to what she was agreeing.

And she wasn't so sure that she wanted to find out.

"So, what are you up to, this fine-but-ridiculously-hot New York night?" Alan asked Chelsea as he stood grinning in her doorway.

She hadn't been expecting anyone. She'd bowed out of going to the movie with her friends so that she could come home and log on to Young Love Online. Karma and Lisha had come home from the movie, which they said was great, and then they'd decided they were still hungry, so they had gone out to the diner on the corner. They promised to bring Chelsea back a burger.

"Not much," Chelsea said, opening the door for him. She kissed him on the cheek. He turned to give her a real kiss, but she eased herself away.

I've really got to talk to him, she thought to herself. *He's too terrific a guy for me to lead on. After all, Nick is breaking up with Jazz, so I've got to just tell Alan the truth.*

But how?

"So, how was your weekend?" Chelsea asked, sitting on the couch. Alan sat down next to her. "I mean, I know I saw you at work this morning, but we didn't get to talk or anything."

"Well, let's see," Alan said, "my cousin in Tenafly is very rich and very boring. She's a senior in high school and the extent of her conversation is guys, fashion, and movie stars."

"That bad, huh?" Chelsea sympathized.

He put his arm around her. "And what's up with you—besides getting reamed out by Bigfoot this morning, that is."

Chelsea laughed. "Who told you her name?"

"Karma," Alan said. "In the lounge. I almost split a gut laughing."

"God, Bigfoot hates me." Chelsea sighed. "She's so vicious."

Alan noticed her laptop computer, which was still on, sitting on the table. "You working?"

"I logged on to Young Love Online," she explained. Then she quickly told him about her show idea, and how it had to be together for Friday.

"Wow, good for you," he said. "So how does this Young Love Online thing work?"

For the next fifteen minutes or so Chelsea gave Alan the guided tour of Young Love On-line, a computer chat service, which, unlike some of the other commercial services, was wholly dedicated to introducing teens to one another. And the best part of it all, it was absolutely free. That was because one quarter of every computer screen was dedicated to an advertisement, which changed every five minutes or so. In fact, at that very moment there was an advertisement for *Trash* on the screen.

"So," Chelsea said as she showed Alan around the service, "this is the wave of the future in how teens are going to meet."

Alan lifted a lock of her hair and tickled her face with it. "I think I prefer the old-fashioned way." He smiled, his voice soft and seductive. "Like how I met Chelsea Jennings."

Chelsea leaned forward abruptly and snapped the computer off.

I really need to talk to him, she thought. *He's such a great guy, I have to tell him the truth, and there's no time like now to do it. About Nick. And me. And us.*

"Alan, I . . . need to talk to you," she blurted out.

"Uh-oh," Alan said. "Bad sign."

"I . . . oh, shoot, I don't know how to do this," Chelsea groaned.

"Uh-oh, again," Alan said. "Okay, hit me with it. I promise I won't cry."

"About me and you," Chelsea added.

"And no one else?" Alan added. "Don't you want to talk to me about you and me and Nick?"

"Did he talk to you?" Chelsea asked hopefully.

Alan smiled, though his eyes were sad. "C'mon, Chels," he said. "I see how you get when you're around him. It's like your IQ drops thirty points. Which still leaves you smarter than the vast majority of the world, I might add."

Chelsea sighed. "You're way too nice for me."

"Well, that kind of comment is always the kiss of death," Alan said lightly.

"I guess I didn't realize that I'm that easy to read."

"You're not," Alan said. "I'm just a good reader. So, you and Nick—"

"I like you," Chelsea blurted out. "I mean, I think you're the greatest, nicest, most terrific—"

"But Nick gives you sparks, huh?" Alan asked.

Chelsea nodded, her head low.

"You give me sparks," Alan admitted. "Geez, aren't we a cliché here. Hey, maybe I could write about our little triangle. What do you think?"

"I don't want to do anything to hurt you," Chelsea said earnestly. "I would never—"

"Chelsea," he said softly, "you can't make a person feel sparks. Can you?"

"No," she admitted, her voice just as soft as Alan's. "I guess you can't."

He hesitated a moment. "I just hope . . . I hope he doesn't hurt you."

"He's breaking up with Jazz," Chelsea said quickly.

"How about the others?" Alan asked.

"I . . . guess I don't know . . . I mean, I'm sure he's breaking up with them, too," Chelsea said, flustered.

"I don't know if Nick is into a one-girl, one-guy kind of thing," Alan said. "I mean, I like the guy. He's my roommate. He's my friend. But . . . I don't know. . . ."

"Don't worry about me," Chelsea said, kissing his cheek.

"Okay." Alan sighed. "You've got to follow your heart, wherever it takes you. Right?"

"Right," Chelsea agreed.

"But we're still friends?" he asked, his gorgeous brown eyes glistening slightly.

"Always," Chelsea said fervently. "Always."

"Then I consider myself a lucky guy," Alan concluded, his voice betraying his Texas roots a little.

He's from the South, like me, Chelsea realized. *I never even thought about it before.*

"I'm lucky, too," she said. "To have a friend as terrific as you."

Alan hugged her, and it was the warmest, best hug she'd ever gotten from a guy friend in her entire life.

She thought about what he'd just said about Nick, but she quickly put any doubts about him out of her mind.

She and Nick belonged together.

Alan was right. She really did have to follow her heart.

Karma barged into Sumtimes's office—this week she was Laura Sumtimes—and triumphantly dropped a six-inch-tall stack of files, newspaper clippings, computer printouts, and magazines on the desk. Chelsea was sitting in Sumtimes's chair, her feet up on the desk, rubbing her eyes with exhaustion.

"Read 'em and weep," Karma said gleefully. "I'm telling you, I have this mass-murderer research thing down cold. If I were Sumtimes, I would be offering me a major raise. So, read!"

Chelsea looked up at her blearily. Karma had on a silver stretch tube dress, silver lipstick, and white go-go boots. Chelsea had on her oldest jeans and a Vanderbilt sweatshirt—she felt lucky to have managed to put on clothes at all.

She was both utterly exhausted and incredibly nervous and excited, from lack of sleep, too much work, and too much caffeine, not to mention the reality that it was fifteen minutes to show time for Young Love Online.

And now Karma wants me to read about mass murderers and their kids, she thought. *Little does she know how close that subject is to my heart.*

"You want me to read this stuff *now*?" Chelsea asked. "I have worked like a dog for five days to get my first show idea on the air, which is going to happen in"—she checked her watch—"fourteen minutes, and you want me to read your research files *now*?" She jumped up from her chair. "I ought to be down there—"

"Relax," Karma said to her, plopping down onto one of the red wet-look vinyl chairs. "I heard Sumtimes get the call from the car phone—your star guest is, like, twenty blocks away in the limo."

"But what if they hit traffic? I'm finished."

"They hit traffic, Sela Flynn will fly to the studio," Karma said. "That's how badly the girl is dying for her fifteen minutes of fame."

"It's not funny," Chelsea retorted. "I've got to have that girl here—"

"Tell you what," Karma said. "I'll stay here until she gets here. If she doesn't show up, I'll go on as her."

"You're a peach," Chelsea said with a smile.

A big laugh came from the television monitor in the corner of Sumtimes's office. All the producers had closed-circuit TV monitors in their offices, directly connected to the *Trash* studio on the ground level. Right now, in the studio, Demetrius, the gorgeous Hispanic guy with the beautiful, long hair whom Chelsea had run into her very first day at *Trash*, was warming up the audience. He picked a girl out of the crowd, stripped off his shirt, and was dancing down and dirty with her to some loud rock music while the audience hooted and whistled their approval.

"That guy is seriously hot," Karma said, watching Demetrius dance on the monitor. "I could be falling in love. Or at least in lust. Gawd, with my luck he'll turn out to be gay. No guy that good-looking is ever straight."

As Karma watched the monitor Chelsea put her head down on the desk again. She thought back on the previous five days—the five hardest days she had ever worked in her entire life.

In the office at seven in the morning, she recalled, *and home after ten o'clock every night. I've been so busy, I haven't even had a chance to see Nick. I made more phone calls than I ever thought possible, ate more delivery Chinese food and pizza than I ever wanted to, and spent more time typing notes into the computer than I ever did on any paper I wrote in high school.*

And the meetings! With Sumtimes, with Barry, with the others . . . but never with Jazz.

And now, here it is. Thirteen minutes to airtime. And my star guest is stuck in traffic.

The show, though, was set. Chelsea—with the cooperation of Young Love Online—had managed to put together five pairs of teen guys and girls from across the United States, Canada, and England, who had been corresponding with one another and "chatting" live on the Young Love Online for weeks or even months.

In most cases, they'd even exchanged photos already, although in two cases *Trash* had to intervene and set up the photo swap. Barry had handled that part of the process.

He's been so great, Chelsea thought. *The only reason I got this break was because of him.*

Barry had made certain that all the show guests were flown to New York first-class and put up in separate hotels, where they were allowed unlimited room service.

And now here they were, thirteen minutes from going on the air. The guests were in separate offices at *Trash*, with the exception of Sela Flynn, from Gallup, New Mexico, who was scheduled to meet Nigel Wynn, from York, England. They'd been writing and "chatting" for several weeks, and according to Chelsea's preshow interviews, she thought they were the couple most likely to really hit it off big in person.

"That guy Demetrius is poetry in motion," Karma said, her eyes still glued to the monitor. "Do you think I should ask him out or what?"

The phone on Sumtimes's desk buzzed. Chelsea picked it up.

"Chelsea Jennings, intern," she croaked. Her voice was weary.

"We're sending Sela Flynn up to you now," the receptionist said. "Barry says to bring her down to makeup at four-twenty P.M., and she's going on the air at four-forty P.M. Got it?"

"Got it," Chelsea said, though it seemed a very short time for Sela to spend in the makeup room.

"Thank God," she told Karma, "Sela's here."

"Told ya," Karma said. On the monitor, Demetrius had finished dancing, and now two guys from the audience were volunteering to dress as hula dancers and dance for Bigfoot.

Karma tapped her perfectly manicured finger on her stack of research. "So, where was I? Oh, yeah, check this out. I've outdone myself this time." She put her hands out in front of her, palms up, on either side of the stack of papers she'd just brought in.

Mass-murderer files.

Word of the upcoming but as yet unscheduled show on the teen children of mass murderers had spread like wildfire around the *Trash* offices. This was another one of Jazz's pet projects, and it seemed as if everyone was working on it, under Bigfoot's direction.

Everyone but Chelsea, that is. So far, anyway.

"The guy that killed and ate all those people in Chicago," Karma said triumphantly, holding up a computer printout. "He had three kids. Two of them are teens. One of them said yes already."

"That's . . . great," Chelsea managed.

"Then," Karma said, pawing through her papers, "we've got a whole fifteen minutes in the works on teen kids of postal workers who've gone berserk." She held up a big magazine article. "See?"

Chelsea got a sick feeling in her stomach. "Uh-huh."

"And Bigfoot's working on the whopper herself," Karma said confidentially. "About sixteen years ago there was this really rich lawyer in some hick Tennessee town—I forget where—who totally flipped out one day and shot up everyone in a Burger Barn."

Chelsea felt nauseated.

"But that's not the kicker," Karma continued. "He went home to off his wife and his kid, and his wife stabbed him in the throat with a butcher knife. Can you deal?"

I am going to throw up. Right here, right in Sumtimes's office. . . .

"His kid, was like, only a few months old, so she'd be a teenager now," Karma continued, "and Roxanne is trying to—" She stopped talking and peered at Chelsea. "You okay? You're getting kind of green. Chels?"

There was a rap at the door. One of the *Trash* security guys stuck his head in. "Chelsea Jennings?" he asked. "I've got Sela Flynn waiting at the elevator. I'll go get her."

"Are you okay?" Karma asked again. She felt

Chelsea's forehead. "You're all clammy! You have the flu?"

"I'm fine," Chelsea lied. "I'm just tired."

"Well, get some rest tonight, sweetie," Karma instructed her. "I'll make you a big pot of home-made chicken soup. It cures anything, and it's the one and only thing I know how to cook."

Chelsea managed a sick smile.

The guard opened the door. Chelsea stood up.

"That's my cue to exit stage right," Karma commented. "Break a leg today."

"Thanks," Chelsea said as Karma and Sela passed each other in the doorway.

"Hi," Sela said shyly as Chelsea got up to greet her.

"Hi," Chelsea said. "I'm really glad to see you!"

Sela smiled at her, and Chelsea tried not to look shocked.

This is one of the most unattractive girls I've ever seen in my life, she thought. *I hoped that it was just that her photo wasn't very good, but she's worse looking in person than she was in the photograph. She's got to be eighty pounds overweight. And look at that bad skin! And the receding chin. And the size of the nose! And that terrible lank, greasy hair . . .*

"So, welcome to *Trash*," Chelsea said brightly. "I'm Chelsea Jennings, and I'll be your host until we get you on the air. Is there anything I can get you? Coffee? Tea? Bottled water?"

"How about a Coke?" Sela asked nervously.

"Diet?" Chelsea asked automatically.

"Regular," Sela answered, "if you've got it."

"Coming right up," Chelsea promised. She went to the little refrigerator next to the TV monitor, picked out a bottle of regular Coke, and handed it to Sela.

The girl opened it and drained half of it in one fell swoop.

"Thirsty," she confessed. "I am so nervous."

Chelsea knew her job was to put Sela at ease. "There's nothing to worry about, I promise you."

"I hope he likes me," Sela confessed. "I mean, everything went so well on-line, but . . ."

"I know, this is a little nerve-racking," Chelsea sympathized.

"I just hope he likes me when he sees me," Sela said, twisting a lock of her dank hair between her fingers.

"He's going to love you," Chelsea promised. "You guys swapped pictures, right?"

"*Trash* did it for us," Sela said, her eyes shining. "He is so cute. Did you see his picture?"

Chelsea nodded. She'd seen pictures of both of them before. Nigel Wynn was as handsome as Sela was unattractive.

"And our last names rhyme!" Sela went on. "That's destiny, don't you think?"

"Absolutely," Chelsea agreed, smiling at the girl.

"I believe in destiny," Sela said seriously. "So

136

does Nigel. He told me that on-line. We've talked over the computer for hours and hours."

Chelsea nodded her encouragement.

"I can really talk to him, you know?" Sela said earnestly. "I mean, we talk about everything. We both love to read Keats and P. B. Shelley poems out loud. We both love politics, and we were both born in September. We both love hot chocolate. He plays soccer—well, he calls it football—and I'm a big football fan. I mean, it's destiny. Isn't it?"

"I guess it is," Chelsea said, a small smile curling at the edges of her mouth. She was beginning to like Sela. There was just something so open and innocent about her, it was, well, refreshing.

"Have you met Nigel?" Sela asked eagerly.

"No," Chelsea answered. "But I've seen his picture."

"And he's seen mine." Sela shook her head in wonder. "Don't you think it's wonderful that he loves the real me? I mean . . . well, I know what guys like. Girls who look like models. And I don't look like a model."

"All guys aren't like that," Chelsea said. "Nigel isn't!"

"I guess not," Sela said with wonder. "How lucky can Sela Flynn get, huh?"

Chelsea smiled at the girl again. *And that's why I saved this story for last,* she thought to herself. *Because it is the most wonderful of all. Most guys wouldn't look at Sela twice, except to make some joke at her expense. But Nigel fell in love with the real Sela. The audience is going to love this.*

"Oh look!" Sela said, pointing to Sumtimes's TV monitor. "It's the show! It's Jazz! Ohmigod, I *love* Jazz!"

Trash was live on the air. Chelsea turned up the volume so that Sela and she could hear Jazz's show intro—Jazz delivered it as she stood, apparently naked, inside a huge Apple-style computer, which covered her body from just above her breasts to just below her crotch.

"Cyber-sex?" Jazz asked. "Cyber-love? Teens falling in love with teens by computer. Is it possible? You're going to see for yourself, as we bring together five teen couples who've never met each other in the flesh, but who've been talking by computer forever. With the help of Young Love Online, you're going to see how love can blossom—or not—in cyberspace!"

The audience applauded loudly, and across the bottom of the screen, a feed from a live "chat" conversation currently under way on Young Love Online scrolled, along with the information number for Young Love Online.

That was my idea, Chelsea thought proudly. *This way, the viewing audience can actually see how the service works.*

After the commercial, Sela watched, transfixed, as Jazz introduced two different couples who'd met in cyberspace. First, she brought out one of the partners, blindfolded that partner, and then brought out the other one. Once the second teen was on the set, she pulled the blindfold off the first teen, who was now seeing the person they'd been writing to for the first time in the flesh.

The meetings were sweet and romantic. Both couples gave each other long, soulful kisses, egged on by the studio audience. Then Jazz waded into the audience to field questions for the couples.

"That's going to be me," Sela said happily. "That's me and Nigel in a little while. This is the greatest day of my life!"

Chelsea looked at her watch. It was four-fifteen P.M., just about time to take Sela down to makeup.

"Okay, Sela," she said. "Are you ready to be a star?"

Sela's grin was so bright that it seemed to light up the room another notch.

"You betcha," Sela replied eagerly. "Do I get my makeup done and everything?"

"By a professional makeup artist," Chelsea promised. "Sela Flynn is about to become a star."

"All right!" Jazz cried. "Let's bring out, all the way from York, England, Nigel Wynn!"

The *Trash* audience applauded, and the applause turned to cheers, whoops, and wolf whistles when Nigel actually appeared on the set and walked slowly across it to where Jazz was standing.

Nigel was drop-dead gorgeous. Over six feet tall, lean and muscular, with brown hair and green eyes, a cleft in his chin, and a boyish, dimpled smile. He was dressed simply, in black jeans, a black jacket, and a white T-shirt.

Taller, better looking Tom Cruise, Chelsea thought, automatically reverting to Karma's habit of comparing everyone with famous people.

"Oh, gosh," Sela breathed, grabbing Chelsea's hand. They were standing in the wings, watching the set. Nigel had been brought on from the other side of the stage. "He's so hot." She turned nervously to Chelsea. "He really likes me?"

"He likes you," Chelsea assured her, giving her hand a little squeeze.

Jazz went over to Nigel and gave him a big hug, which he returned with enthusiasm. Then they both sat on the couch. Next to them were the inflatable man and the inflatable woman, upside down.

"Maybe I oughta trade in my current model for this guy," Jazz quipped, and the audience cheered.

"So, what's a great-looking guy like you doing flirting in cyberspace?" Jazz asked him.

Nigel shrugged. "You can meet some great people," he said, in his soft British accent. "Like Sela."

"You really like her, huh?" Jazz asked eagerly.

"She's fabulous," Nigel said. "Sometimes I feel as if I dreamed her up, she's so terrific."

The audience awwwwwed its approval, and Jazz smiled.

"You're a sensitive guy, right, Nigel?"

"I like to think so."

"I mean, you're not into surface things, right? You look at a girl's soul, right?" Jazz asked earnestly.

"Absolutely," Nigel said firmly. "That's what's so great about meeting on-line. You get to really know the person before looks even enter into the picture!"

Jazz nodded in agreement. "So, you ready to meet Sela?" Jazz asked.

"Absolutely," Nigel said, standing up.

"Oh God, oh God, this is it—" Sela yelped.

"Cool," Jazz said in her laconic style. She took the big red blindfold out of her back pocket and tied it around Nigel's eyes. Then she took Nigel by the elbow and guided him to the middle of the set, putting him in front of the four other "cyber couples" who'd been united for the first time on the *Trash* set.

"Let's bring out"—Jazz was reading from one of the *Trash* file cards she always seemed to be holding—"from the happenin' burg of Gallup, New Mexico, Miss Sela Flynn!"

A recording of the old Chuck Berry rock standard "I'm So Glad I'm Livin' in the USA" started playing, and Chelsea gave Sela a gentle tap on the arm.

"Get out there!" she commanded gently.

"Wish me luck!" Sela murmured. Then she took a deep breath and ran onto the set, prompting a huge reaction from the live audience. There was a mixture of cheering, whooping, and catcalls.

Jazz greeted Sela warmly as the music stopped. She waited for the crowd to hush, as it did, following the signs that read QUIET, PLEASE that were flashing all over the set.

"So, Sela Flynn," Jazz asked Sela, casually slipping her arm around her, "what do you think of Nigel Wynn?"

"He's so gorgeous!" Sela said honestly. "Hi, Nigel!"

"Hi, Sela," Nigel said from behind his blindfold. "You've got a great voice."

The crowd cheered and hollered some more.

"So, are you ready for his blindfold to come off . . . so that he can see you for the very first time?" Jazz asked.

"In person, you mean," Sela said eagerly. "I'm ready!"

Jazz went over to Nigel and, with great ceremony, yanked the blindfold off of his eyes.

"Sela Flynn," she announced, "meet Nigel Wynn!"

The crowd cheered loudly. But Jazz had been too slow. As soon as she had taken off the blindfold, Sela had made a quick move toward Nigel, enveloping him in her massive arms and pressing her body against him, even as Jazz got her last sentence out.

It was just what all the other couples had done.

Except, unlike the other couples, Nigel pushed Sela away.

Hard.

"What is this?" he sputtered. "Is this some kind of a joke? This isn't Sela Flynn. Who is this *thing*?"

Sela just stood there, now five feet away from Nigel, in complete shock.

What's going on? Chelsea wondered frantically. *What's happening? Of course that's Sela!*

"It's Sela Flynn," Jazz assured Nigel.

"No it's not!" Nigel exploded. "Sela Flynn has blond hair, and blue eyes, and high cheekbones. And she's slender. And tall. This girl is some . . . some . . . dog!"

The audience started whooping and hollering, and from the rear of the studio, some people started making barking-dog noises.

"You sent me her photo!" Nigel accused Jazz. "This isn't her! What kind of stunt are you people pulling here?"

Oh God, Chelsea thought, putting two and two together. *It's a setup.* Trash *sent Nigel a picture of some other girl—some beautiful girl—saying that it was Sela. Sela probably never described herself to Nigel on the computer. They did this—no, Barry did this—to embarrass this girl.*

143

This is the most horrible thing I've ever seen.
And there's nothing I can do about it.

"But . . . but it's me," Sela said miserable, her face red and blotchy with embarrassment. "You know, both with September birthdays, both of us like poetry."

"Look, I'm sorry," Nigel said stiffly. "You're not what I expected. I mean—"

"Why, Nigel," Jazz said mockingly, "I guess you're more shallow than you thought, huh?"

Jazz turned to the number-one camera as the cameraman, with Sky holding the cable for him, came in for a close-up of her face.

"So," she continued, "we see the truth. You think beauty is more than skin-deep? You think that we don't judge books by their covers? You think that looks don't count? Look again, everyone. Look again."

She glanced over at Nigel and Sela, both miserable. The camera pulled out to take in the two humiliated people, then came in tight on Jazz again.

"So, hey, guys, the next time you think of yourself as a real sensitive dude, you might want to think again," she said coolly.

"It's all image. It's all a game. You think you'll look like you do now forever? Even I won't look like this forever. It's disposable, we're all disposable. Poof. Bye-bye. Nothing lasts, know what I mean? But, that's what makes it *Trash*, doesn't it? So, until next time, may all your days—and especially your nights—be TRASHy."

The red light on the number-one camera clicked off.

The show was over.

The studio audience stood up and cheered as Jazz took a bow.

Slowly, Chelsea made her way onto the set, to collect Sela Flynn, who still hadn't moved.

"Come on," she said to Sela gently, putting her hand on the girl's arm. "I'll help you get a taxi back to your hotel."

Sela turned and looked at her, her eyes wounded and betrayed. "I thought you were nice. . . ."

"I swear to you," Chelsea said, "I had no idea that Nigel didn't have your picture. I would never, ever have done that to you . . . or to any-one."

Sela just stared at her. Then, like a whipped dog, she let Chelsea lead her off the set of *Trash*.

C helsea just stood there in front of the *Trash* offices, staring at the taxi with Sela inside as it pulled away.

I can't believe it, she thought. *I just can't believe what Barry did with my show idea.*

"Wanna buy a pretzel? A hot dog?" The vendor standing next to her grinned a hopeful grin at her.

"No," she said tersely. She didn't want food. She wanted to wring Barry Bassinger's neck.

Chelsea turned on her heel, marched back into the building, where she took the elevator to the third floor, and marched right past Barry's new secretary—a voluptuous brunette version of Anna Nicole Smith—barging into his office.

"Barry—"

His back was to her. He swung around. He was on the phone, and he motioned for her to have a seat.

"Yeah, yeah, sounds cool," he was saying into the receiver. "Go with the guy whose mom shot up the shopping mall in Idaho, nix the babe whose brother poisoned the Jell-O at Fort Bragg—we'll do siblings of mass murderers another time, okay? Glad to see you're on top of it, Roxi."

He hung up the phone. "Chelsea, great to see you! Did you meet my new secretary, Olyvia? She just started this morning."

"No, I—"

"Listen, Roxanne told me that kids-of-mass-murderers idea came from a nine-hundred call off your tape," Barry said. "Lemme tell you, it's going to be killer—hottest show we've ever done."

"Barry, I—"

"I'm gonna tell Roxi you're free to help with the research now, okay? You're not all tied up with the marriage-to-Jazz thing, are you?"

"Barry, my show—"

"Oh yeah, it was great, wasn't it?" he said. He locked his hands behind his head. "You got your first one under your belt now, kid."

"How could you do it?" Chelsea yelled, jumping out of her seat. Her hands were trembling. She clenched them into two fists of rage at her sides.

Barry looked at her coolly. "You seem upset."

"How could you do that to my show idea?" she cried. "I worked my ass off, I haven't slept in five days, you told me you loved my idea, and then you . . . you—"

"And then I made it into something that would attract a *Trash* audience," Barry finished mildly. "You know, Chelsea, people are actually tuning in. Which is how we make money. Which is how we stay on the air. Or did you think this was social work?"

Chelsea took a deep breath. "No. I did not think this was social work. But you screwed me and you know it—"

"I don't recall getting any closer to you than a couple of drinks at the Empire," Barry said, a smug smile on his face.

Tears stung Chelsea's eyes. "You mean you did this to me because I didn't . . . because I wouldn't go to your apartment with you?"

"Hey, don't flatter yourself," Barry said. "Sure. I wanted to get up close and personal with you, shall we say. But New York is full of pretty girls who are more than willing to spend time with me. You weren't interested—hey, that's the way it goes."

"But then why—"

Barry came around his desk and leaned on the edge. "Sit down," he told her.

"I don't want to sit down."

"Do it anyway," Barry said mildly. "I'm your boss."

She sat.

Barry folded his arms. "Let me explain the facts of life to you, Chelsea. TV is not some magical thing. It's not so complicated. We put on a show. If lots of people watch a show, the advertising time on that show is sold for more money. The show makes more money, the station makes more money, everyone makes money. It's really that simple."

"But . . . but what about *morals*?" Chelsea demanded. "What about *integrity*?"

"What about it?" Barry asked. "I happen to be very proud of what I do. It's great entertainment. What, you think everything Shakespeare did was so highbrow?"

"You set Sela up," Chelsea said, her voice low and tense. "You humiliated a perfectly innocent girl on national television—"

"Oh, come on," Barry interrupted. "It was at least as big a goof on that pompous jerk Nigel whatever-his-name-was. 'I don't care about looks, I love the real Sela,'" he mimicked with a fey British accent. "Please! What a *schmuck*! Guess we blew his little facade, huh?"

"But Sela—"

"Don't worry, Chelsea," Barry said. "I guarantee you that this experience will be the highlight of Sela Flynn's life. One day she'll tell her grandchildren about the time she was on national TV—"

"You're wrong," Chelsea said. "You just . . . you crushed her, Barry. I can't believe you don't see it. I can't believe that you can rationalize using people like this—"

"Let me ask you a question," Barry said. "How many TV internships did you apply for?"

Chelsea's face immediately blushed a bright red. "Wha . . . what do you mean?"

"I mean how many?" Barry asked.

"A few," she said, her cheeks burning.

"Give me a number," he said.

"Okay, a lot," Chelsea said, her voice low.

"And Chelsea Jennings, Queen of Integrity, picked *Trash*. My guess is, you didn't end up with a whole lot of options, am I right?"

The silence in the room was all the answer he needed.

"Right," Barry said, answering himself. "Hey, don't feel bad. The comp out there is a bitch. So, here you are at *Trash*, the only place where your nice-smart-girl-with-great-grades ordinariness made you stand out from the crowd." He smiled at her. "You knew exactly what kind of a show this was, right?"

"Right," Chelsea admitted tersely.

"So, why did you do it?" Barry asked, spreading his arms wide. "I'll tell you why. Because you wanted something and you wanted it bad—a chance to get into TV, right? Your only chance, is my guess.

"Well, everybody wants something, babe. You're no different than anyone else. You wanted to use *Trash* to launch your TV career, but now you want to go all holier-than-thou about the kind of stuff we do."

Barry brought his face close to Chelsea's. "Face it, Chelsea, it's all TRASH. That's the whole point. Everything and everyone is disposable. Including you. Including me. So we might as well ride the ride while the ride is good, you know?"

Chelsea stood up with what she hoped was a shred of dignity. "You're right, Barry. I knew what *Trash* was when I applied for this job."

Barry nodded. "I like you, Chelsea. You're a sweet girl. And you're smart. A little naive, maybe, but hey, that's kind of refreshing. So, you ready to go help with the mass-murderer research?"

"What I need," Chelsea said slowly, "is to get out of here."

"A little breather?" Barry asked. "Sure. Take a walk by the Hudson. I'll tell Sumtimes to expect you back, in say, forty-five minutes, okay?"

"I'm not coming back today," Chelsea said. "I have a lot of thinking to do. If you want to fire me, go ahead."

"Don't do anything stupid, okay?" Barry told her. "Don't blow your gig here—"

"I need to think about everything you said," Chelsea said. "And I need to figure out what kind of person I really am."

She turned and walked out the door.

"Mom? Hi, it's me." Chelsea sat on her bed, the phone cord wrapped around her pinky finger.

"Chelsea! Are you okay?" came her mother's concerned voice.

"Sure," she assured her mom. "I just wanted to call you."

"But it's six o'clock New York time," her mother said. "Didn't you tell me that you usually work until at least seven?"

"I got out earlier today," Chelsea said. "How's everything in Nashville?"

"Just fine," her mother said. "We started a summer choir at school, about twenty girls. We're going to put on a Fourth of July concert."

"That's really nice, Mama," Chelsea said softly.

"Honey?" her mother said. "You don't sound right."

"I'm fine," Chelsea said, trying to keep her voice light. She wrapped the phone cord more tightly around her pinky. "Mama, how come . . . how come we never talk about what happened with Daddy?"

Silence.

"Mama?"

"I can't talk about that now," her mother said quickly.

"But we never talk about it," Chelsea said.

"And I see no reason to start now," her mother said, her voice cold. "What's gotten into you?"

"It happened," Chelsea said softly. "You pretend like it didn't, but it did."

"Maybe it didn't," her mother said. Her voice sounded weird. "Sometimes I think it was just some terrible dream I had. And that's just the way I plan to keep it."

Chelsea shut her eyes. She was so tired.

"Now, honey, are you taking your vitamins?" her mother said, her voice back to normal. "Because you can get terribly run-down."

"I'm taking vitamins," she assured her mother.

"And get enough rest, Chelsea," her mother continued. "You don't do well if you get less than eight hours, sweetheart."

"I know, Mom," Chelsea said.

"Well, I don't want to run up a huge long-distance bill," her mother said. "You should wait and call me when the rates change, sweetheart."

"I'll call you again soon, Mom," she promised, and carefully hung up the phone.

Then she lay down on her back and stared up at the ceiling.

Who am I, really? she wondered. *What kind of person am I?*

Barry was right. I am just using Trash. *Maybe everyone really does use everyone. Maybe I'm just as bad as everyone else.*

There was a knock on the door.

She padded into the living room and opened the door without even checking to see who it was.

It was Nick.

"Hi," he said. "I was staring out the window

in my apartment and I saw you walk into the building."

Chelsea sat on the couch. She put her head in her hands.

"Hey," he said, sitting down next to her. "What happened?"

"I hate my life," Chelsea said.

He put his arm around her. "You want to talk about it?"

She turned her head to look at him. "No. I want to talk about us. Did you break up with Jazz?"

"Is this an inquisition?" Nick asked uncomfortably.

"No," Chelsea said. "I didn't mean it to come out like that." She leaned her head on his shoulder. "Did you see my show today?"

"I haven't been in," Nick said.

Chelsea sat up. "Did Jazz fire you?"

"Nah," he said. His hair was loose, and he looped it behind his ear on the right side. "So, how did your show go?"

"Horrible," she said, and quickly told him what had happened. "I mean, this girl, Sela, was humiliated, totally humiliated. It was a horrible, cruel thing to do."

"Sounds like it," Nick agreed. "But you have to wonder . . . why would anyone agree to be a guest on *Trash*? I mean, Jazz pulls stuff like that all the time, you know?"

"I guess that's true," Chelsea agreed. "So, okay, people like the chance to be on TV. And they like the trip to New York, and the ritzy hotel and everything. But that doesn't make it right to exploit them, does it?"

"No," Nick said. "But they have some responsibility, too. It's like . . . like everyone is using everyone."

"Oh, God, that's what Barry says," Chelsea said with a sigh. "But I don't believe the world is like that—"

"Not everyone," Nick said, his voice low.

She leaned her head against his shoulder. "Not you," she whispered. He stroked her hair. "Well, at least now that my show is over, we'll be able to spend time together."

"Good," Nick murmured.

"That is, if you broke up with Jazz," she added.

"Didn't you just ask me that?"

"Yeah, but you didn't answer me." She lifted her head and looked at him. "You're afraid you'll lose your cushy job, is that it?"

"I was all set to break up with her, okay?" Nick said. "And she probably would have fired me. But this morning she broke up with me first."

"She did?"

"She met some French actor who's in town doing the new Danny DeVito flick. She told me I could take the rest of the day off to lick my wounds."

Chelsea smiled and kissed his cheek. "We lucked out."

"Yeah," Nick said, but his voice sounded guarded, flat.

A feeling of dread tightened Chelsea's throat. "You don't sound happy."

"Look, Chels, I think you are fantastic—"

"Oh, God, this is the same talk I had with Alan—"

"No, no, I'm not blowing you off," Nick assured her. He pushed his hair off his face again. "I want to see you. I want to be with you. But . . ."

"But . . . what?" she asked, gulping hard.

Nick got up and paced to the window, where he stared out at the street. "I'm not ready for some . . . some big commitment or anything."

"Who said anything about a big commitment?" Chelsea asked.

"That's the kind of girl you are," he said, turning around and leaning on the windowsill.

"Oh, thank you for explaining that to me," she said sarcastically. "I don't recall our 'big commitment' conversation—"

"Come on, don't get all bent out of shape," Nick said. "I just mean we should be able to see who we want, and be together as much as we want—"

"In other words, we'd be free to see other people," Chelsea translated.

"Well, yeah," Nick said nervously. He walked back over to her and lifted her to her feet, then he stared into her eyes. "Can you go with that, Chels?"

"Can I go with that," she repeated. "Well, let me tell you how I feel. When you really care about someone, you don't want to 'go with that.' When you really care, you want to only be with that person, and it hurts your heart if that person is with someone else—"

"Come on, Chels—"

"No, you 'come on,'" Chelsea said fiercely. "Can't you make a commitment to anything? You couldn't commit to college and you can't commit to a relationship, either."

"That's cold, Chelsea, don't be like that—" Nick began, reaching out for her.

Chelsea stepped backward, wrapping her arms around herself. "This is how I am, Nick. I'm not going to let you push me and pull me— like one day we're together and the next day there's some other babe. I didn't realize just how perfect you and Jazz really are for each other."

He reached out for her again. She moved away.

"Bye, Nick."

"But—"

"Bye. Have a nice life."

A muscle twitched in Nick's jaw. He opened his mouth to say something, then closed it again. Then he turned and walked out.

Chelsea dropped onto the couch. The only sound in the apartment was the omnipresent hum of life in New York City—sirens, taxis, buses on the street.

"Mama," Chelsea whispered under her breath. She began to rock back and forth, still holding herself, as if she was afraid she would dissolve into a million pieces if she let go.

And then the tears came.

L isha walked into the apartment two hours later, and followed the sounds of sobbing to Chelsea's room.

The door was open. She was in there, crying, and flinging things into the open suitcase on her bed.

"Chelsea?" Lisha whispered from the doorway.

Chelsea didn't respond. She just kept crying and throwing stuff into her suitcase.

"Chels?" Lisha said, louder now. "What's going on?"

"I hate it here," Chelsea said between sobs. She pulled some T-shirts out of her drawer and threw them into her suitcase. "I can't stand it anymore. I'm going home."

Lisha walked over to her and gently pulled the denim shirt Chelsea was holding out of her hands. Then she sat her on the bed and sat down next to her. "What happened?"

"Everything happened," Chelsea cried. She plucked a Kleenex from a box on her night-stand and blew her nose loudly. "Did you see my show today?"

Lisha shook her head no. "Bigfoot had me stuck in the Xerox room all afternoon, and there's no monitor in there. Didn't it go well?"

"Ha," Chelsea snorted. "It was a huge hit, a big success. Everyone loved it."

"So then, what's the problem?" Lisha asked.

Chelsea quickly and bitterly told her what Barry had done to her show. "I hate him," she finished, blowing her nose again. "I hate all of them—Jazz, and Roxanne, and Barry—Barry most of all. And then I came home, and—"

"We having a pj party?" Karma asked, coming into the room. She was carrying a grocery bag. "I bought a chicken to make you soup," she told Chelsea, then she saw the open suitcase and Chelsea's tearstained face. "Oh, God, someone died," she guessed, putting down her bag of groceries with a thud.

"Nobody died," Chelsea said. "My life died."

"What happened?" Karma asked, joining the other two on Chelsea's bed.

"Did you see her show this afternoon?" Lisha asked.

"Nah, I got stuck at the public library on Forty-second street doing mass-murderer research. What, it was a disaster?"

Lisha filled her in.

"Why, that scheming low-life little twerp of a producer," Karma seethed.

"I guess we were right about Barry wanting to get into your pants," Lisha said dryly. "Not that I have any satisfaction in saying 'I told you so.'"

"But you know what?" Chelsea said. "He would have done what he did anyway. I could have been his new girlfriend and he still would have changed the show behind my back. That's how he is. I see that now."

"It's so underhanded," Karma said, shaking her head.

"I didn't even get to the worst part," Chelsea said, grabbing another Kleenex. "I got back here, and Nick stopped over and . . . and we broke up." Fresh sobs burst from her throat.

"Wow, that was the quickest torrid relationship in history," Karma said.

"What happened?" Lisha asked.

"Jazz dumped him," Chelsea said bitterly, her voice nasal from crying. "Lucky him—that meant he never did have to break up with her, and he got to keep his job at *Trash*.

"And then," she continued, "then he told me he really liked me, but of course he didn't want anything heavy, so we should both be able to see other people."

Karma and Lisha were quiet.

"So . . . so I broke up with him," Chelsea said. "Alan was right about him. He's a two-timing lowlife and I'm better off without him."

"Alan said that?" Karma asked, surprised.

"No," Chelsea admitted. "But he did tell me that he didn't think Nick was ready for a real relationship—same difference."

"But, Chels . . ." Lisha began carefully. "Don't get mad, but . . . I mean, what's so bad about starting out your relationship with Nick slowly?"

"Whose side are you on?" Chelsea demanded.

"I'm on your side, of course," Lisha said. She blew her feathered bangs out of her eyes. "But you guys don't even really know each other yet. I mean, what's so terrible about getting to know each other before you decide you and Nick are this big, exclusive thing?"

"He's just a big flirt," Chelsea said. "What, I'm just supposed to let him be with me on Monday, and some other girl on Tuesday, and maybe I'll see him one night of the weekend if he can fit me in—"

"But, Chels, you act like he has all this power," Karma said. "Like poor little you would be sitting by the phone dying for him."

"Well, I would be," Chelsea confessed.

"But you could be seeing other people, too," Karma pointed out. "It's a two-way street. And in my experience, when the traffic is going both ways, the little guy car ends up wanting the little girl car all that much more."

Chelsea and Lisha just stared at her.

"Okay," Karma said, "maybe I didn't put it that well. The point is, if you act like you're all

164

needy and desperate, that always drives a guy away, pronto."

"Needy and desperate?" Chelsea exclaimed. "Just because I'm mature enough to want a commitment?"

"Maybe you just need to give him a little more time," Lisha said. "Believe me, I know what happens when you let a guy be everything, the be-all and end-all of your life. I did it. It sucked."

"When?" Chelsea asked, wiping her eyes with her Kleenex.

"When what?"

"When did you do it?" Chelsea asked. "You act like you don't care about guys at all. You barely give Sky the time of day, and he's darling and smart and nice and crazy about you."

"Let's just say I . . . had a bad experience, okay?" Lisha said, her voice low.

"Here's what I suggest," Karma said, biting her lower lip thoughtfully. "You call Nick up, you tell him you want to talk. Then you tell him you've decided you really want to see other guys, so actually his idea is great, and—"

"But I don't feel that way!" Chelsea objected. "I don't want to play all these games! I don't even know how. All I want is a nice, normal, committed relationship between two people—"

"Well, if you ask me, Nick is too hot to throw away because his time frame doesn't fit yours," Karma said, folding her arms.

"It's more than that," Chelsea insisted. "He made it pretty clear he doesn't really care about me. It's over."

"But—" Lisha began.

"And *Trash* will be *Trash* if I never go back there," Chelsea continued. Her eyes swam with tears again. "And I can't. Go back."

"Oh, Chels—" Lisha tried again.

"No, listen," Chelsea said. "Barry was right. I'm a total hypocrite. I really did just take the summer internship because it was a way to get into television. I knew the kind of show *Trash* is. So I have no right now to bitch about it." She stood up and looked out the window, at the street scene below that she had actually grown to love.

Two African-American teenage boys were throwing a basketball back and forth as they walked along. A young couple walked hand in hand, laughing together about some private joke. The Arab hot-dog vendor on the corner, with his gold front tooth, handed a hot dog to a little girl as her elderly grandfather handed the vendor some money.

I'll miss that part of it, Chelsea thought, *all the different people and sights and sounds of New York.*

She turned away from the window. "I don't belong here," she announced.

"So, you're just . . . quitting?" Lisha asked. "Just like that? No notice, nothing, just walking out?"

166

"It's not like anyone will care." Chelsea sniffed.

"I guess you just couldn't cut it," Lisha said sharply.

"How can you say that to me?" Chelsea cried. "I did everything for that show today—everything! And then Barry—"

"So what?" Lisha asked. "And Nick didn't fall into line just the way you wanted him to—well, so what to that, too."

"Lisha, come on—" Karma chided her.

"No, she needs to hear this," Lisha continued. "When we were kids, I worshiped you. Do you know that? You were so much prettier than me, and so much more popular, so much cooler, that I was grateful every single day that you hung out with me.

"I always thought: Chelsea is going to have a really fantastic life. I just pretended that I was going to be a rock star because I thought it sounded so cool. But I knew it was never going to happen. But you . . . you really *were* going to be this famous journalist, and you'd live in all these exotic cities. You'd have romances and you'd win journalism prizes, and you'd be totally fearless."

Lisha cocked her head at Chelsea, then she laughed a short, cold laugh.

"Well, I guess I was totally wrong about you. You had me fooled. I never thought you were the kind of girl who would fold just because things got tough. But I was totally wrong. You're just a cute, sweet, ordinary girl from Tennessee, who wants a cute, sweet, safe, ordinary life—"

"You don't know what you're talking about!" Chelsea cried, jumping up from the bed.

"Oh, you guys, don't do this—" Karma began.

"If you only knew how funny that is—" Chelsea said.

"I have eyes, Chelsea," Lisha said. "I see the open suitcase—"

"There's nothing so terrible about wanting an ordinary life—" Karma tried to interject.

"The two of you know *nothing*!" Chelsea shrieked. She felt manic, crazed, out of control. "You are utterly clueless!"

"Look, all I'm saying is that everyone doesn't have to be Jessica Savitch," Karma said. "Remember her? She was this great investigative reporter and then there was this big scandal about her life—"

"Big scandal?" Chelsea echoed, her voice shaking. *"Big scandal?* I'll tell you what a big scandal is! I've lived with this big scandal my whole life, and neither of you know anything about it!"

Lisha and Karma stared at her, confused, waiting.

"Oh, right, Lisha, you thought you knew me so well." Chelsea sneered. "But you didn't know *anything*!"

She whirled around to face Karma. "Remember that guy that Roxanne is investigating? That mass murderer in 'some hick town in Tennessee"? The rich lawyer who shot up all those innocent people in a Burger Barn? And his wife who stabbed him with a kitchen knife to save the life of her baby?

"I'm the baby! That's me! That's who I really am!"

Lisha and Karma's jaws both fell open in silent shock.

Chelsea buried her face in her hands, sobbing so hard that she thought her heart would break.

Other than that, the room was deathly silent.

"Is this . . ." Karma finally began slowly, "is this a joke?"

Chelsea just kept sobbing into her cupped hands.

"My God, she's telling us the truth," Lisha realized. "You are, aren't you?"

Chelsea nodded yes into her hands.

"And I never knew a thing." Lisha marveled.

"No one knew," Chelsea said, still sobbing. "No one knows now, except me and my mother . . . and now the two of you. Oh, God, I'm gonna be sick."

Chelsea ran into her bathroom and heaved into the toilet. When she could lift her head she saw Karma and Lisha standing in the doorway.

"Go away," she moaned. "Please, just go away."

She bent over the toilet again, gagging and heaving.

And then she felt a soft, comforting hand stroking her back, so softly. "It's okay, Chels," Lisha said. "Let it all out."

Karma ran water from the sink into a glass and held it out to Chelsea. "Just take little sips," she cautioned.

"You don't have to be nice to me," Chelsea mumbled, her head resting wearily on her arms.

"That's true," Lisha said. "But we're going to, anyway."

"Here, drink," Karma said, making sure Chelsea took the water.

She took a small sip. "Are you . . . are you scared of me now?" she asked in a small voice.

"Oh, yeah," Karma said, her tone gently sarcastic. "Petrified."

"How could I ever be scared of you?" Lisha asked. "You're my best friend."

"Mine, too," Karma added. "What can I say?" she continued teasingly. "The three of us have bonded like sisters."

"You can't mean that—" Chelsea began.

"Of course we can," Karma said. "I've never had friends like you guys in my entire life. You think a little thing like a psycho-killer father is going to deter me?"

Chelsea laughed a little. "Don't make jokes about it."

"Why not?" Karma said. "It beats crying."

Chelsea got gingerly up from the floor of her bathroom. She rinsed her mouth with some

Scope, then Karma and Lisha helped her back into her bedroom. She sat on her bed, Lisha on one side of her, Karma on the other.

"God, Chelsea, how did you and your mother keep it a secret all these years?" Lisha asked.

"She pretends it never happened," Chelsea said, reaching for another Kleenex. "I only know the details from the old newspapers up in our attic. I know Mom changed her hair color, and she got glasses—I guess so she wouldn't be recognizable. And of course she changed our last name—"

"Kettering," Karma recalled from her research. "That was your name, right?"

Chelsea nodded.

"The world is so bizarre." Karma marveled. "I mean, what are the odds that you'd end up working for *Trash*, and we'd be researching your family for a story?"

"Didn't you once tell me that you didn't move to Nashville until you were three?" Lisha recalled.

Chelsea nodded. "Mom told me that a long time ago. I don't know where we were, between the time I was ten months old and the time I was three."

"Relatives?" Karma guessed.

"There's my mother's sister," Chelsea said. "In Detroit. I don't know."

"And your mom won't talk about it at all?" Lisha asked.

Chelsea shook her head no. "You know my mom. You'd think she was the most 'normal' mother in the world."

"God, it's so hard to believe." Lisha shook her head in wonder. "Your mom, of all the people in the world, seems least likely to . . ." She let the rest of her statement trail off.

"What I want to know is how could you bear to carry this around by yourself all these years?" Karma asked. "I would have lost it!"

"I was afraid to tell anyone," Chelsea said, her voice low and ashamed.

"But you didn't do anything!" Lisha exclaimed. "You were an innocent little baby!"

"I know," Chelsea said. "I've told myself that a thousand times. But then I thought . . . my father seemed normal. Totally normal. That's what all the newspaper articles said. He wasn't crazy. He wasn't depressed. Just some weird chemical thing happened in his brain one day, and he turned into a monster." She gulped hard and twisted the Kleenex in her hand. "Sometimes . . . sometimes I have kind of a temper tantrum and I fly off the handle. And then I think . . ."

She was shaking so hard she could barely get the words out.

"And then I think," Chelsea managed, "what if it's genetic? And what if it happens to me, too?"

Tears streamed down her face. "Oh, God," she sobbed, "it's just so horrible."

Karma and Lisha both hugged Chelsea as she cried bitter, scared, pent-up tears. She cried and cried until she felt as if there was nothing left inside of her.

"I'm so sorry you felt like you couldn't tell anyone," Lisha said. "And I'm so sorry about what I said before."

"Forget it," Chelsea said. She took a deep, shuddering breath. "Well, anyway, I'm not sorry I told y'all now. I mean, it's scary, but I'm not sorry. Just promise me that you'll never, ever tell anyone."

"Promise," Lisha said.

"Double-triple promise," Karma added.

"So, I guess now you can see why I'm leaving," Chelsea said. "I'm not about to wait around for Bigfoot to slip the noose around my neck."

"We'll just have to make sure she doesn't find out who you are," Lisha said.

"But she's so relentless—" Chelsea began.

"Relentless, maybe," Karma cut in. "But, frankly, the three of us could outsmart her and only use half our brain cells. She's not nearly as hot shish kebab as she thinks."

Chelsea smiled at her. "Thanks, but . . . I'm still leaving. It's all over with Nick, and I'd be a hypocrite if I stayed at *Trash* and helped create *Trash* every day."

"Listen, I feel that way sometimes, too," Lisha admitted.

"You do?" Chelsea asked, surprised.

"Not at first," Lisha said. "I told myself this is a dog-eat-dog world, so I might as well be the big dog on the porch. But, I don't know, lately it's really been getting to me."

"Yeah, me, too," Karma agreed. "So what if this gig helps me become the next Ted Turner? I mean, my mother always says you lie down with dogs, you get up with fleas."

Chelsea laughed. "My mother says the same thing."

Lisha threw herself back on the bed and stared up at the ceiling. "Too bad we can't sabotage from within, huh? Or wait, even better, do something that exposes the true trash behind the public *Trash*—"

"Oh, my gawd, that's brilliant!" Karma cried, jumping off the bed.

"What?" Lisha asked, sitting up. "It was just wishful thinking."

"But it doesn't have to be!" Karma exclaimed. "What if . . . what if we made a film? Behind the scenes at *Trash*? A secret film—"

"Showing how ugly and backbiting it is," Chelsea continued, "how exploitive—"

"Time out," Lisha said, making a T-sign with her hands. "Just how are we supposed to accomplish this feat? 'Uh, excuse me, Bigfoot? Would you mind if I just film you while you lie, cheat, and sleep your way to the top?'"

"Not very subtle," Karma agreed, pacing

Chelsea's room. "Here's how I see it. We get equipment from Sky—he's got great connections, right? We film secretly, we hide the camera. It can be done, I'm telling you!"

"You really think?" Chelsea asked slowly.

"Of course!" Karma insisted. "I'm telling you, the brainpower in the room could do just about anything!"

Chelsea smiled. "And you always claim you aren't smart."

"So sue me, I lied," Karma said. "It's a cute little affectation of mine."

"You know, we really could do it," Lisha realized. "It's so wonderfully underhanded . . . and so *just*! We just turn the tables on them—I love it!"

"And it's so much more satisfying than slinking home with your tail between your legs," Karma told Chelsea.

Chelsea smiled. "It's so, so . . . *Trash*!"

"And I've got the title!" Lisha cried, a huge grin on her face. "*My TRASHy Summer*!"

"It's perfect," Chelsea admitted.

"Brilliant," Karma agreed. She turned to Chelsea. "So, you'll stay?"

"You will, won't you?" Lisha added. "Come on, we'll be the three underground Musketeers, one for all and all for one."

"I just can't believe—" Chelsea began. She gulped hard. "I can't believe that now that you know the truth about me that you still . . . still

175

want to be friends with me. I mean, I always imagined this scene where people would run away screaming."

"Chels," Lisha said, "everyone has secrets, you know? Stuff that they hide from the world, stuff that makes them afraid that if anyone knew, people wouldn't like them anymore."

Chelsea stared into Lisha's eyes. "Something happened to you in Europe, didn't it?" she said. "Something bad."

Lisha nodded. "And I will tell you—both of you—one day. I promise. I'm just not ready."

"Well, my life is an open book," Karma said in her nasal whine. "Unless you count the fact that I was adopted from Korea when I was three, and I don't know anything about who I am or where I come from."

"So . . . I'm not the only one with secrets, huh?" Chelsea said in a small voice.

"Right," Lisha agreed. "Although admittedly yours is a whopper."

All three of them laughed.

"Okay, you guys," Karma said, reaching out a hand to Chelsea and a hand to Lisha, and trying, with all ninety-two pounds of her body weight, to lift them from the bed.

They both got up, and the three stood in Chelsea's room, hand in hand in hand.

"Now it's the three of us against the world," Karma announced. "Can I get an *amen*?"

"Amen!" Chelsea and Lisha cried.

"And here's to *My TRASHy Summer*," Lisha said with conviction. "*Trash* is about to meet the enemy . . . and it is us!"

"It's show time," Lisha said laconically, taking the headphones off her head and rubbing her ears. "Man, these things hurt after a while."

The clock on the wall read four P.M. Lisha, Karma, Chelsea, and Alan had all been stuck transcribing 900-number phone calls for the past three hours.

"Time for today's *Trash*," Chelsea said, also pulling off her earphones.

"Monday, July first," Alan said with satisfaction. "Circle it on your calendar, folks. The first day of work on that soon-to-be infamous underground video, *My TRASHy Summer*."

"Shhhhh!" Chelsea hissed, looking around nervously. "Someone could hear you!"

"There's no one here at Sicko-Central but us interns," Alan said. Sicko-Central was the name they had given to Room 401, where they seemed to spend half their time, transcribing the often bizarre 900-number phone calls.

"We diabolical, underhanded, wait-until-the-whole-world-sees-our-film interns," Karma added with satisfaction.

"Right now, right this minute, a tiny camera, courtesy of Sky, is running, hidden behind some books in Bigfoot's office, aimed right at her chair," Alan said smugly.

Alan had volunteered to come in extra early to plant the camera. It was a complete success. "Trash-cam in place," he'd reported proudly.

Chelsea smiled at her friends. She could hardly believe how much better she felt than she had felt on Friday.

For one thing, telling them my secret feels like this huge, heavy load has been lifted off my chest, she realized. *To think that they know the truth, and they still like me. It's . . . it's just so incredible!*

And then there's all the plotting we've been doing for My TRASHy Summer, she thought, a smile playing around her lips. *If we can pull this off, it will be the most satisfying thing I've ever been a part of in my entire life.*

The three girls had spent the weekend plotting their strategy for *My TRASHy Summer.* They had to have Sky in on it so that he could arrange to get them video equipment and editing space.

It wasn't hard to convince him, and on Sunday he had stopped over with a top-of-the-line video camera, which he showed them how to use. He also told them that a friend of his dad's with a studio in Brooklyn would let them use the editing room and equipment for free, providing the space wasn't booked by paying customers.

After that, they all agreed to tell Alan, and he had been just as enthusiastic as the other four of them.

Sunday afternoon, as they were all sitting around the girls' apartment, plotting just where and how to begin secretly filming the next day, and eating pizza, Nick had stopped over to see Chelsea. Everyone but her wanted to let Nick in on *My TRASHy Summer,* but she had been adamantly opposed and she had won.

Chelsea had gone out into the hallway to talk with Nick, but it didn't seem to her that he really had much to say. The conversation was terse and awkward, and finally Nick had just gone back across the hall to his own apartment.

I'm totally over him, Chelsea told herself. *I'm really glad it never went any further than it went.*

"I'd rather be here than on the set," Karma commented, interrupting Chelsea's thoughts. Karma took her headphones off. "Better company."

Nonetheless, she turned up the volume on the remote control so that the three of them could see what the *Trash* subject of the day was going to be.

To make their lives somewhat more pleasant, Sumtimes—whom Chelsea was actually, sort of, coming to like—had put a TV monitor in Sicko-Central so they could keep an eye on the show in the late afternoon.

"Okay, dudes and dudettes," Jazz was saying, after the audience had finally finished cheering her entrance. For some reason, she was dressed today, from head to toe, in black plastic garbage bags. The inflatable man and the inflatable woman were clad in the same material, and were sitting on the coffee table.

"So, guys," Jazz continued, "who here thinks that their after-school jobs totally suck?"

The audience went crazy.

"Big duh, right?" she asked. "I mean, flipping hamburgers, stuck in the stockroom, mowing people's lawns, taking care of their screaming kids, all for chump change. So what would you call it?"

"It's trash!" the audience yelled gleefully.

And that answer is written for all of you on huge cue cards that Demetrius is holding up right now, Chelsea thought cynically.

It was the truth. Chelsea had seen this drill before. When Jazz wanted the audience to respond as one in a certain way, she had Demetrius or Bigfoot drill them on their responses during the warm-up, and then had cue cards containing the appropriate response held up at the appropriate moments.

"You know it," Jazz agreed. "So today, we're

bringing you six teens who all think their after-school jobs bite the big one. They're ready to tell their bosses, on nationwide TV, to take that job and shove it."

The refrain from the old country music song "Take This Job and Shove It" played for a few seconds on the studio sound system while the audience cheered again.

"But wait, there's more!" Jazz continued. "What are they going to do for money now, you may ask?"

"What are they going to do for money?" The audience chanted obediently, reading from another off-camera cue card.

"She's an artist," Karma said, watching Jazz on the monitor. "A sick and demented person, but an artist."

Jazz walked up a level on the set, to the three girls and three guys picked to be on the show. They sat there, grinning at her. One of them waved to the camera.

"What are they going to do for money, now that they're telling their bosses off?" she asked. "Well, these are six teens who'll do anything—and I do mean *anything*—for money! And we're gonna watch 'em do it! Why? Because we're all TRASH!"

"I can't take it," Karma said, snapping off the monitor with the remote control. "I'm going to get some coffee. You want?"

"I'll go with you," Lisha said.

Chelsea looked at the piles of cassette tapes she still had to transcribe and shook her head. "I'd better stay and work on these, y'all," she said, "or else I'll be here all night."

"Tell you what"—Alan got up and put his hands gently on the back of her neck—"I'll go get you some coffee and, say, a buttered bagel, and I'll bring it back here for you, okay?"

Chelsea smiled up at him. "You're nice."

"That's true," he said, smiling back at her. "Back in a flash."

"If you lose your mind, you come find us in the lounge," Karma called.

Chelsea turned back to her headset and computer keyboard. She put the earphones back on, faced the computer keyboard, and pressed the play button on the tape console.

"Hiya, Jazz!" a young voice with a definite California beach feel to it said. "I'm Lydia Lazinsky from Long Beach, California, and I think it would be too rad to do a show about teen girls who've broken up with their boyfriends, but now the girl wants to prove how much she wants the dude back, even if the guy, like, cheated on her or abused her, or something, because—"

Chelsea pushed the pause button.

"Lydia, you need two years of intensive therapy," she said, shaking her head. She rubbed her eyes, which burned from too many hours staring at a computer screen.

I guess I will go just join them in the lounge,

she decided, getting up to stretch. *There's only so much I can take.*

Chelsea had just stepped into the hallway when Sumtimes came running up to her at full speed. There were beads of sweat on her bald head.

"Thank God I found you, thank God, thank God," Sumtimes said, the words rushing out of her mouth. She clutched at the sleeve of Chelsea's white cotton sweater.

"Are you talking to *me*?" Chelsea asked, totally bewildered.

"Come with me," Sumtimes demanded, and she pulled Chelsea with her down the hallway.

Oh, no, they found the video camera in Bigfoot's office and they think I did it, Chelsea realized with dread. *There goes my job, there goes My TRASHy Summer, there goes my professional reputation forever.*

"Come on!" Sumtimes screamed. "Move it!"

Maybe if I insist that I planted that camera all by myself, Chelsea thought, *maybe if they believe I acted alone, the others won't lose their jobs.*

"Look, I can explain—"

"Just shut up and run!" Sumtimes yelled over her shoulder. Chelsea followed her, thinking she would turn into Bigfoot's office, but to her surprise Sumtimes ran down three flights of stairs and into Studio C.

And when Chelsea finally, breathlessly, ran inside the studio, it was totally apparent what the problem was.

And it had nothing to do with a hidden video camera.

There was a teen girl on the set, but she wasn't one of Jazz's six take-this-job-and-shove-it guests.

She was an unattractive, overweight teen girl with a big nose and lank, greasy hair.

And she was holding a pistol to Jazz's head.

Chelsea recognized her immediately.

It was Sela Flynn.

"Okay, Sela," Chelsea said, her voice very shaky, her legs feeling like Gumby legs beneath her. "Here I come. Just take it easy, okay?"

"Get out here, Chelsea!" Sela yelled at her. "Get out here, now!"

"Just take your time, kid," a New York City hostage unit cop's voice said into Chelsea's earphone. "Take just one step at a time. And for God's sake, be careful!"

Chelsea gulped hard. "I'm coming, Sela," she repeated. "I'm coming out now."

Slowly, so slowly, with the encouraging voice of the cop from the hostage unit in her ear, she approached Sela Flynn.

The whole thing felt like a terrible nightmare.

Sela obviously hadn't gone back to New Mexico. Instead she had hung around New York all weekend, and then had managed to become a part of the studio audience of the day's show. She'd found a seat in the back row. And just as soon as the first commercial break ended, and Jazz had put the camera on the first teenager who was about to tell her boss to take her job and shove it, Sela had burst out of her seat and run down the aisle, waving her gun in the air. She ran onto the set, right up to Jazz.

At first, everyone had laughed, thinking that the whole thing was just TRASH.

But then, Sela had fired her gun at the ceiling, blowing a large hole in the acoustic tiles.

After that, it was pandemonium. People were screaming, crying, diving for cover under the seats of the studio.

There was a panicked run for the exits, but Sela had pulled the microphone off a white-faced guest and had yelled into it: "Lock the doors now, or I'm shooting Jazz! And I have five sticks of dynamite strapped to my right leg, under my jeans. I can blow this whole place up, and I'll do it, too!"

The doors had been quickly locked.

Then Sela made the rest of her demands.

She wanted twenty-five people from the staff of *Trash* brought in, and she wanted them to sit on the floor in front of her. This had to happen within three minutes. If there weren't twenty-five people sitting on the floor in front of her in three minutes, she'd shoot Jazz.

Staff members had quickly been dragged into the studio, among them Karma, Lisha, and Alan. Sky had already been in the room with a cameraman, and he, too, was sitting among the twenty-five hostages. While this was happening Sela yelled into the microphone that if one person who was already in the room tried to escape, she'd shoot Jazz.

She didn't want to see any police. If she saw a cop, she'd shoot Jazz.

She wanted everything that was going on to be broadcast live, and she wanted a TV set up within five minutes so that she could see that it was all being broadcast. If it wasn't live on the air, she'd shoot Jazz.

And she only wanted to talk to one person— one person to be the go-between, between her and the police who were sure to arrive soon.

That person was Chelsea Jennings.

"The only sane person around here!" Sela had screamed wildly into her mike, which she had clipped to her flannel shirt. "I want Chelsea!"

If Chelsea Jennings didn't show up within five minutes, Sela had sworn to shoot Jazz. And if anyone else tried to approach her, or talk to her, or even get within ten feet of her without her permission, she'd shoot them, too.

Right after that, Chelsea recalled as she walked slowly toward Sela, someone stuck an earphone in her ear so that she could hear from the police SWAT team that was set up outside the studio doors.

"Sela," Roxanne said, slowly getting up from her spot with the other staff members on the floor in front of the furious teen.

Chelsea froze, still twenty feet from Sela.

"I'm on your side, Sela," Roxanne said sweetly. "I know just how you feel, and I want you to know I'm going to arrange for you to be Jazz's special guest on a show next week—"

"Really?" Sela asked. She seemed to be considering the offer.

"Oh, yes," Bigfoot said, putting one large foot in front of the other as she approached Sela. "I can do it, too. I'll make sure that—"

Wordlessly, almost casually, Sela turned to Roxanne, aimed her gun, and shot her in the right foot. Bigfoot fell to the stage.

Everyone began screaming, but Sela screamed into her microphone loudest of all. "Just put a tourniquet on her foot and shut her up. I didn't shoot to kill. Believe me, I know how to shoot to kill."

She looked over at Chelsea, her eyes pleading. *Oh, God, please don't let her shoot me,* Chelsea thought as Alan and Sky lifted Roxanne and carried her to the corner to apply first aid. "I'm right here, Sela," she said in what she hoped was a low, calm voice.

"She didn't follow directions," Sela told Chelsea.

"That's right," Chelsea said soothingly.

"You're doing great, kid," a cop said in her ear. "Talk to her calmly. You're the only one she'll talk to."

As she continued to walk sooooo slowly toward Sela, she saw Karma and Lisha looking up at her from their places on the floor. She saw the fear in their eyes.

Fear for her.

Please, God, she prayed, *don't let me die now. Now that I finally feel like I'm not alone anymore.*

Sela had her gun pointed at Jazz's head. Her hand was shaking. Chelsea was within five feet of her now.

"Take it easy, kid," the cop's gruff voice said in her ear. "Remember, she's nuts."

It was all Chelsea could do not to talk back to the voice in her ear, but she knew that would drive Sela absolutely wild—that she, Chelsea, had a direct line to a New York City Police Department SWAT team.

"That's close enough," Sela snapped.

Chelsea stopped walking. "Here I am, just like you asked for."

"Are we live?" Sela asked.

Chelsea pointed to the TV. "See for yourself. We're live," she said. "All across America."

Sela grinned a sick grin. "Good," she muttered. She leaned into the microphone clipped to her shirt. "Testing, one, two, three, testing." Sela grinned again at Chelsea. "That's what professionals say when they test their mikes."

"You want to know why I'm here?" Sela asked Chelsea, her voice reverberating through the studio.

"Yes," Chelsea said.

"I want her tied up, first," Sela said, nudging her gun at Jazz.

Chelsea spotted a couple of electrical cords a few feet away, lying in the aisle. She walked over and picked them up.

"You!" Sela yelled, pointing the gun at Alan. "Tie her up."

"Okay," Alan agreed. He took the cables from Chelsea and quickly bound Jazz's wrists and ankles. Jazz helped by holding her hands and feet out for him.

"Sit back down with the others," Sela barked at him.

Obediently, Alan found his place again next to Karma and Lisha.

"Get her talking," the cop said in Chelsea's ear. "Get her to confide in you."

Chelsea only prayed that Sela couldn't hear the cop, too.

"So," she said, "you're live on the air coast-to-coast. What do you want to say . . . so that we can let some of these people go?"

"Good, kid!" the cop said in Chelsea's ear. "That's perfect. Keep it up."

"She humiliated me," Sela said, her voice low and hurt. "Jazz humiliated me. How can I go back home now? How can I? Don't you think everyone I know saw the show? Don't you think they're all laughing at me now?"

"I'm sure Jazz is sorry," Chelsea said, hoping that it was the right thing to say.

"Yeah?" Sela said. She pointed the gun at Jazz's ear. "Say it," she commanded Jazz. "Are you sorry?"

"I'm sorry," Jazz said.

Sela laughed hysterically, wiping her eyes, teary from mirth. "You must think I'm as stupid as you are. I know you're not sorry. Big duh, as you always say, Jazz. You're only sorry that now I have the power, and you don't."

"I really am sorry," Jazz said fervently.

"Sure." Sela sneered. "We'll see how sorry you are. We'll see how sorry you are when I keep you tied up here, for as long as I want." She swung her head to look at Chelsea, her eyes wild. "I want her humiliated like she humiliated me!"

"Tell her she's the boss," the cop whispered in Chelsea's ear.

"You're the boss, Sela," Chelsea said. "*Trash* is your show now. I'm here to help you run it."

The seconds stretched into minutes, the minutes into hours. It was now six forty-five P.M., and Sela was still holding the studio hostage. And the hostage drama was being broadcast live, coast-to-coast.

Not only was it on the stations that normally picked up *Trash* in syndication, but it was also on CNN, Headline News, and large chunks of the drama were being shown on all the major-network nightly news broadcasts.

Sela had asked for a live hookup with one of

the networks, and she'd received what she'd asked for. Now, Ted Masterson, the nationally known and very handsome news anchor, was asking her questions, which she was answering.

During all this, Jazz lay at her feet, bound, while Sela held court from the middle of the studio and Chelsea stood by her side.

"I mean, tell me, Ted," Sela was saying, "why is it that a girl like Jazz gets her own TV show, and all that money and fame? Why not me? Huh?"

"I don't know, Sela," Ted Masterson said, in his deep, sonorous tones. "Why do you think?"

"Because she's tall and thin and gorgeous, you moron!" Sela spat out. "Don't play dumb with me! What, you think you're a news anchor because you're so smart? Don't make me laugh. You look like a movie star, that's the only reason!"

"Uh-huh," Ted agreed gravely.

No one saw the trapdoor on the studio floor— which led to a crawl space full of cables and electrical equipment—open just a few inches behind the spot where Sela and Chelsea were standing.

Moments later it opened a crack more.

Then, so slowly, a few inches more.

That's when Chelsea saw, behind Sela, the top of Nick's head as he inched out of the crawl space.

Their eyes met. Sela didn't see him. She was too busy staring into the camera, ranting on.

Quickly, Chelsea turned her eyes back to Sela.

"I mean, that's all America cares about, right?" Sela ranted on. "Come on, Ted, try and tell me different!" She focused on camera number one, as if it were the news broadcaster himself. "You can't, you dumb-ass, because—"

She stopped suddenly and stood stock-still. Perhaps she'd felt a gust of breeze on her bare ankles from the slightly opened trapdoor behind her.

She whirled around. She saw Nick's head.

"No!" Chelsea screamed.

Nick lunged, reaching out to grab Sela's feet from behind, evidently hoping to trip her up and knock her to the floor.

"No!" Chelsea yelled again.

Sela fumbled a moment, then fired her gun at the trapdoor, as it slammed shut with a loud bang.

Some people were screaming, others crying, whimpering, and moaning.

"What the hell happened in there?" the cop was yelling into Chelsea's ear. "The angle of the camera sucks. Chelsea? Kid?"

Oh, God, she shot Nick, Chelsea thought, fear clutching her heart. *He's down in the crawl space, wounded, maybe dying, oh, God.*

I can't let Nick die.

And then, without giving herself time to consider the insanity of it, while Sela was still breathing hard, her gun pointed shakily at the trapdoor to the crawl space, Chelsea made her move.

Like a football lineman trying to deliver a vicious sack to a hapless quarterback, she took a flying leap, and landed on Sela's back.

The two of them fell to the studio floor, and the gun flew harmlessly away from Sela, skittering across the floor like a hockey puck.

In an instant fifteen people converged on Chelsea and Sela as the two of them wrestled on the floor of the set.

Thirty arms held Sela down.

Bedlam reigned on the set as the doors to the studio burst open and three dozen policemen, wearing flak jackets and helmets, ran through the open doors and onto the set. Quickly and efficiently, they handcuffed Sela and hustled her away.

Wordlessly, Lisha and Karma hugged Chelsea tight.

"Get me out of these damn cords," Jazz yelled. She was still helpless, tied up in the electrical wires. Sumtimes quickly began to untie her.

"Wow, is all I have to say," Alan said, grabbing Chelsea up in his arms. Sky came over and hugged her, too. "You're a hero, Chels."

Just then, Barry, who had made sure he was nowhere in sight of the studio during the ordeal, entered and ran over to Chelsea. "You were fabulous!" he cried, hugging her hard. "So fabulous!"

It felt as if a zillion people were surrounding Chelsea, and flash cameras were going off. It was pandemonium.

"I have to find Nick!" Chelsea yelled, tears streaming down her face. "We need an ambulance! She shot him! He's down in the—"

And then she felt warm lips on the back of her neck.

She turned around.

Nick.

"I thought you were—"

"She missed," he said, and enveloped Chelsea in his strong arms, pressing her face into his chest.

"You were an idiot," Chelsea said softly.

"The thought of something happening to you . . ." Nick said gruffly. "For two hours I was stuck under the stage, in the crawl space. I was running wires down there when all this started. So I waited. Then I saw the trapdoor. Then I waited some more, until her foot covered a hole in the floor by the trapdoor. Then—"

"I thought she shot you," Chelsea said, holding him so tight that her knuckles were white against his flannel shirt.

"Chels," he murmured. "Chelsea . . ."

They just held each other, their eyes closed, realizing what they meant to each other, realizing what they had almost lost, before it had ever really begun.

"Hey, Chelsea?" Barry Bassinger said, sticking his head in between hers and Nick's. "Listen, Larry King's office is on the phone. Can you do his show live at nine tonight? With Jazz? His office just called, and they say they'll send Ted Turner's jet—"

Chelsea just stared at him. More camera flashes went off in her face.

"And then can you do *Good Morning America* tomorrow, six-thirty?" Barry continued. "You and Jazz? The *Today* show? *CBS This Morning*? Jesus, kid, take your pick! The phone's ringing off the hook already!"

"Snap ratings are in, Barry," Demetrius called from the wings. "We just beat the O.J. verdict!"

Barry punched the air in triumph. "Chelsea," he said, "I'm a genius for bringing you in with us. A genius!"

Someone tapped Chelsea on the shoulder.

It was Jazz.

"I wanted to thank you," she said softly. "You saved my life."

"Thanks, Jazz," Chelsea said. Nick's arm was still around her shoulders.

"No," Jazz said, "thank you, uh . . . Chutney." She looked from Nick to Chelsea, and back at Nick. "You make a cute couple," she added.

Jazz walked away, adjusting her clothes and her hair, and went over to the number-one camera, which apparently was still broadcasting live.

"Okay, Jazz," some producer called from the wings. "We go live again in five, four, three . . . !"

Chelsea and Nick watched, astonished, as Jazz automatically counted off the last two seconds silently and looked into the camera, turning on her charm.

"Well, well, well, gang," she said lightly, looking into America's living rooms, "where were we before we were so rudely interrupted?"

Everyone in the studio just stood and cheered.

13

"**W**ell, well, well, gang, where were we before we were so rudely interrupted?"

A close-up of Jazz's face filled the TV screen in the girls' living room. The six friends sat there, along with Belch the dog, rapt, and watched a replay, on a late-night network news special, of the drama that they had lived out earlier in the evening.

"This is truly the weirdest experience of my life," Karma said, her eyes riveted to the screen.

The camera went to Darla Dunnings, a reporter, who was standing on the street, just outside the *Trash* studio. "So, there you have it, Ted. The alleged perpetrator, Sela Flynn of Gallup, New Mexico, is now in police custody. This is Darla Dunnings. Back to you in the studio, Ted."

The camera went to Ted Masterson and his coanchor, Kate Pride.

"What an incredible story," Kate said, looking over at Ted. "I'm sure our viewing audience would like to know what it was like for you, Ted."

"Well, as you know, Kate, Sela Flynn specifically requested that I speak with her on the air, which I did, for an hour," Ted intoned, his voice filled with self-importance. "I found her to be a surprisingly intelligent young woman, actually. But clearly deeply troubled."

"Big duh, Ted!" Lisha yelled at the TV.

"Just incredible, Ted," Kate said again. She looked at the camera. "This is Kate Pride—"

"And Ted Masterson—"

"Wishing you good night."

Alan reached for the remote control and clicked off the set.

They had all been watching TV for the past two hours—ever since they'd managed to get home from *Trash*. Over and over again, on station after station, they had seen their lives played out on TV, with Chelsea making her flying leap at Sela to save the day.

Every station was calling her a hero. Every station was trying to get more information about who she was, where she lived, and just why it was that Sela Flynn had asked for her in the first place.

Chelsea had turned down all the offers to appear on the news broadcasts.

In fact, after calling her mother to assure her that she was all right (Lisha and Karma had called their parents from the guys' apartment), she had unplugged the phone so that no more reporters could get through. Nick had given Antoine the doorman twenty dollars to keep the reporters out of the building, and for once Antoine seemed to be on top of things.

Outside the window, Chelsea could still hear the noise on the street, where hordes of reporters were gathered, waiting for her to come out so they could interview her.

Sky got up and peered out the window. "Yep, they're all still out there, all right," he said. "Like ants at a picnic."

"You realize I can never leave this apartment," Chelsea said.

"They'll move on to the next instant, trashy scandal soon," Alan promised.

"I wish they'd just leave me alone," Chelsea said.

Lisha and Karma caught her eye, and both nodded with sympathy.

They know what I'm worried about, Chelsea thought. *What if some enterprising reporter really digs deep and finds out who I am?*

"I wonder if the Trash-cam got anything good in Bigfoot's office before all hell broke loose," Sky said.

"Sky!" Lisha cried, tilting her head toward Nick, who was sitting on the floor next to Chelsea, holding her hand.

"Oops," Sky said, chagrined. "I forget he didn't know."

Nick scratched at his chin, and Belch leaped up and licked his face. "Hey, Belch," he told the dog, "I got a feeling there's a secret going on that we didn't get let in on."

"I'm sorry, man," Sky said. "We should have told you." He looked over at Chelsea. "I'm sorry, but we should have. We're all in this together, okay?"

Chelsea looked over at Nick. "Okay," she finally said. "He earned it today." And then she told him about *My TRASHy Summer*, and the Trash-cam that they had planted in Bigfoot's office.

"Whoa," Nick said. "Diabolical."

"We like to think so." Karma smiled.

Nick scratched his chin again. "So, the idea is, we take the very medium that they're using to make a mint by humiliating people, and we use it against them and expose them for the petty, ugly, little despots they really are."

Chelsea grinned. "What a smart guy."

"A smart slacker," he corrected her, kissing her cheek. "I think it's great. Count me in."

Chelsea kissed him back, on the lips. "Cool," she whispered.

"Of course, we're stuck in this apartment forever," Nick added. "I don't know how any of us is going to get to the office in the morning to get the camera."

"It's still in Bigfoot's office, even as we speak,"

Alan said smugly. "Although I guess it ran out of tape by now."

"So, tomorrow I leave really early," Sky said. "I don't think I was on camera enough for the vultures downstairs to know I work for *Trash*. And I'll get the camera, reload 'er, and set it up in, say, Jazz's office?"

"Perfect," Lisha said.

They all agreed.

"You realize," Sky continued, "that if we get caught, we'll lose more than our jobs. I mean, forget a career in TV for any of us, because our reps will be shot."

They were all quiet for a moment.

"You know, sometimes you just have to stand for something," Nick said slowly.

"I thought you didn't believe in anything," Chelsea said.

"Guess you don't know me all that well yet, after all," Nick said softly.

Chelsea stood up, and reaching for Nick's hand, she led him into her bedroom and closed the door, to the good-natured catcalls of their friends and yelps of protest from Belch. Then she turned to him.

"I want to tell you something." She took a deep breath. "You were right. I . . . I pushed too hard for some kind of big commitment from you when we barely knew each other. There's a lot about me you don't know . . . things that made me afraid—"

Chelsea stopped. *Am I ready to tell him my big secret?* she wondered. *No, not yet. I need time. And he needs time. But maybe someday . . .*

"Anyway," she continued, "I know that sometimes I kind of . . . fly off the handle. I kind of have a temper," she admitted.

"I noticed," Nick said, a smile playing at his lips.

"The thing is," Chelsea continued, "I really do care about you. And . . . and I want us to get to know each other. So if you still want to be with me—"

"Oh, Chels," Nick murmured. And then his arms were around her, and his lips were on hers, and he kissed her until she felt breathless and giddy with happiness.

"Hey, celebrity!" Karma called from the living room. "If the two of you still have your clothes on, get back out here! Bigfoot is on TV, live from her hospital bed. It's a scream!"

Chelsea and Nick ran back into the living room. There was Roxanne, propped up in a hospital bed, her makeup perfect, her huge cast sticking out of the bottom of the bed.

". . . and I always knew that Chutney was the perfect intern for *Trash*," Bigfoot was saying. "We really value her. She's smart and fearless—everything that *Trash* is all about."

"Get me the hurl sack!" Karma squealed.

"Will you be back at *Trash* soon?" the reporter asked Roxanne.

"Oh, yes," she replied, turning on a photogenic Sharon Stone smile. "I'll be back on my *feet* in no time!"

This sent gales of laughter around the room. In fact, the six of them laughed so hard that they were crying.

"Stop, stop," Lisha cried, holding her stomach. "I can't take any more!"

"You guys," Karma finally managed, "I don't want to get too mushy about this, but you guys are incredible. And this TRASHy summer is turning into the best summer of my entire life."

"And it's only just begun," Chelsea said, her eyes shining. She took in the faces of her five friends, who had become so dear to her, in such a short time.

I am so lucky, she thought. *I am the luckiest girl in the world.*

She smiled at all the faces in the room, all of whom were smiling back at her, in friendship, in love.

It was going to be one unbelievable, incredible, and totally trashy summer.

THE TRASH CAN

Hey Readers,

To those of you who know us from our Berkley series *Sunset Island* or our other series, and to those new readers who've never read a book by us before, welcome to *Trash*.

Trash is wild, huh? And set in New York City, where we met, fell in love, and married. (Veteran readers know that we now live in Nashville, Tennessee.) We've never written anything quite like *Trash* before. But Chelsea, Lisha, Karma, and the guys are already a part of us. And, we hope, a part of you.

You may not know this: *we are the authors who do write back.* So if you want to tell us what you think about *Trash,* or about anything else, write away! A self-addressed, stamped envelope will help speed our reply. We've read thousands of letters over the years from your sister readers, and three walls of Cherie's office are covered top-to-bottom with readers' photos. E-mail? Send to authorchik@aol.com on America Online.

We'll print some excerpts from some letters in upcoming *Trash* books, beginning with *Trash: Good Girls, Bad Boys.* But if you want what you write to stay private, just tell us. So tell us news, tell us your own TRASHy moments, tell us anything! If you want some *Trash* sister penpals, we'll try to set you up with some, too.

How TRASHy it is!

Cherie and Jeff

If you enjoyed *Trash,* you won't want to miss the next book in the series . . .

Love, Lies and Video

Here is an excerpt from the exciting new novel available from Berkley Books.

"**O**h, shish kebab," Karma muttered. It was her favorite anticurse, trying as she was to cure herself of swearing.

By mistake, she had pushed the MESSAGE button on the console in front of her. She sighed. Once the intro message got started, there was no way to cut it off until it was over. So she listened to it again.

"Hey, this is Jazz," Jazz's voice said coolly. "Thanks for calling 1-900-I'M TRASH! That's right, it's your chance to be with me, Jazz, live on TV, coast-to-coast, and now in Holland, Argentina, and Australia, too! Just tell me why you should be on my show—your TRASHy show idea. Leave your name, address, and phone number, too! If you're under eighteen, get your parents' permission—big duh. This call costs you just a buck ninety-nine a minute. Go for it at the tone!"

Sicko-Central, how do I love thee? Karma thought glumly.

Karma was sitting alone in Sicko-Central. Sicko-Central, which was what Lisha had nicknamed the room, was the control room for the special 1-900-I'M TRASH! phone number. The 900 number allowed *Trash* viewers, for the price of a dollar ninety-nine a minute, to call in to the show with their best show ideas.

All the interns spent an inordinate amount of time listening to and transcribing the thousands of phone calls that poured in every week. They dutifully wrote down each idea, no matter how weird, and passed them on to the senior producers, usually either Lydia Sumtimes (whose first name changed every week—last week she'd been Julia) or to Bigfoot Renault.

They were also supposed to highlight what they considered great show ideas, which was exactly where Bigfoot had found her kids-of-mass-murderers show concept.

For the moment Karma was at Sicko-Central alone. Chelsea was out picking up Barry Bassinger's dry cleaning and special-order Jamaican coffee beans, and Lisha was out walking Jazz's two matching dalmatians. As for the guys, Karma had no idea, though she had seen Nick disappear into Jazz's private office as soon as he'd arrived that morning.

And I'd thought she'd broken it off with him, Karma had thought. *Of course, it might be nothing. Jazz might not even be in there. I hope it's nothing. . . .*

Karma reached over and pushed the PLAY button.

"Hi, Jazz!" said a male voice. "This is Kenny Bright. I live in Mankato, Minnesota, and I really want to talk to Chutney Jennings. Hey, Chutney, did anyone ever tell you that you look just like Alicia Silverstone? You could be her sister! I'd love to get a date with you. Maybe Jazz can set it up or something. If you like farmers, that's great, because my dad raises corn and I sometimes help him. I'm eighteen, and here's my number. I'd sure like it if you'd call sometime."

Karma typed quickly as she listened. It was the third call that morning asking for a date with Chelsea. For the moment it seemed as if Chelsea were as popular as Jazz herself, who'd received only one marriage proposal so far that morning.

Karma went on to the next call.

"Hello, *Trash,* this is McCloud Crichton, the rock-and-roll manager. Listen, one of my clients—I'm sure you'd recognize who—wants to book Chutney Jennings to be in their next video. They think she looks just like Alicia Silverstone, and Alicia is asking mega-bucks these days. Listen, these guys won't take no for an answer. My butt is on the line here! So if you have a shred of human dignity, you'll return my call. Please?"

So what do I do with this one? Karma wondered as she transcribed the call. *Who knows? But I'll jot the number down for Chelsea, in case she wants to make some extra money. Although I don't think rock videos are exactly her thing. Maybe I'll give the number to Lisha instead.*

Karma went on to the next call. It wasn't about Chelsea for a change.

"Hello, *Trash,* here's why I should be on your show," another male voice said. "Because I have a foolproof method of ripping off the phone companies, and I want to give it to every teen in America. But I'll only appear with a mask and a wig on. If you're interested, call my—"

A pair of hands covered Karma's eyes. Big, sexy hands.

"Your hand is bigger than my entire face," Karma said, turning around.

Demetrius grinned his easy smile and looked down at Karma. She felt even tinier than usual, with him standing and her sitting way, way down below him. She was looking straight at his belt buckle.

"That's better than the greeting you gave me last night," Demetrius told her, sitting down next to her. "Though not by much, I'd have to say."

"Uh, Earth to Demetrius," Karma said. "I didn't see you last night."

"Oh, come on," he said.

"Come on, what?" she asked, bewildered.

Demetrius laughed. "One of the many things

I like about you is your sense of humor. But you could have said hello to me last night."

Karma blinked slowly. "This is a very strange conversation, big guy. Let's review, shall we? We had lunch together yesterday. It was really fun. But last night I was at my apartment giving myself a manicure. See?" She held out her freshly manicured, pale nails.

"Pretty," Demetrius commented. "But obviously it didn't take you all night."

"Why am I not tracking this conversation?" Karma asked.

He laughed again. "You're good."

"True," she said. "I always agree when someone says I'm good, but I still have no idea what you're talking about."

"Last night?" Demetrius asked, his face amused. "I came up behind you on Broadway, about nine, when you pretended you didn't know me? Ring any bells?"

"Not a one," Karma replied.

"In fact, you told me that you're used to being approached by guys, but usually they take no for an answer."

Karma reached out and touched his hand. "That wasn't me. I wasn't on Broadway last night."

"Come on . . ."

"I swear!" she insisted.

"Right," Demetrius said. "I believe you. No, I don't. If it wasn't you, who was it?"

Karma shrugged. "You know us Americans," she quipped, "we all look the same."

Demetrius cocked his head at her. "Is this for real?"

"Yeah. It must have been some other Asian-American fox with a great personality and a fantastic sense of fashion."

"Hmmmm," Demetrius mused. Clearly he still didn't believe her. "Well, what I wanted to ask you last night was when I could see you again."

"You're seeing me now," Karma told him with a grin.

And to think I was afraid to even open my mouth around him, she thought. *Now I'm even flirting with him!*

"You know what I mean," Demetrius said with a look of exasperation.

"Is this a charming Greek-Spanish way of asking someone out?" Karma asked.

"Something like that," he said.

"Here in America, we usually call a person up on this thing called a telephone," she explained.

"Yeah, but somehow asking you here in Sicko-Central seems more appropriate," he said with a laugh.

"How did you know we call it that?" Karma asked.

"Nothing stays hidden for long here at the *Trash* bin," Demetrius replied.

Ha. Shows what you know, Karma thought. *We're making the exposé video of all time about this place, and it's going to stay a big, fat secret until we're ready to show it to the world.*

"Does it ever bother you, working here?" Karma asked suddenly.

"Where did that come from?"

"All thoughts are connected in my head," Karma explained. "So, does it?"

"I don't think this is the time or the place to talk about it, actually," Demetrius said. "I mean, we're on their dime, right?"

"You have a point," Karma conceded.

"Anyway, are you trying to change the subject? Wasn't I just asking you out?"

"No, you were asking some other girl who looks like me," Karma said.

Demetrius groaned and started to get up, but Karma stopped him. "Wait, wait, I'll be serious. Yeah, I'd love to go out with you. I consider it my patriotic duty, what with tomorrow being the Fourth of July and everything."

Demetrius looked at his watch. "I've got to get back downstairs. We're having a meeting about new show warm-ups. So, how about tonight?"

"Tonight?" Karma asked. "Isn't that a little rushed? What if I already have a date?"

"Do you?"

"No," she admitted.

"Good," Demetrius answered, shaking his long hair off his face. "That means yes?"

"You know Jimi's?" Karma asked.

He nodded. "Who doesn't?"

"I work there until one-thirty."

"How about I meet you after work and we go to Around the Clock?" Demetrius asked. "Over on Third Avenue?"

"I know it," Karma said. "Their coffee is beat but it's a date. It *is* a date, right? Or is it too late?"

"Hey, tomorrow's a holiday," he said easily. "And I have a feeling you're worth waiting for. I would have asked you last night on Broadway, if you'd been kind enough to acknowledge that you knew me."

"Mistaken identity," Karma suggested. "Maybe you've been reading too many mystery novels or something."

"I don't read mysteries," Demetrius said. "I think you were just playing hard to get."

"Moi?" Karma asked. "I'm telling you, it wasn't me."

"Oh, yeah, right," Demetrius said with a laugh as he headed for the door. "Believe me, Karma, there couldn't possibly be two of you in this world." He waved.

"I'm going to take that as a compliment," Karma called to his retreating form.

She put her hands behind her head and smiled. "Yeah," she said out loud to the empty room. "Like I would really play hard to get with Demetrius Raines."

She pushed the ON button on the computer

and got ready to type. But a niggling thought stayed with her.

If he really likes me so much, how could he possibly mistake someone else for me? she thought. *How?*

TUNE IN TO THE WILD NEW SERIES BY THE BESTSELLING AUTHOR OF *SUNSET ISLAND*—YOU COULD WIN A TV/VCR! FILL OUT AN ENTRY FORM TODAY!

No purchase necessary. For complete details see below. To enter the drawing, fill in the information below and return it to:

THE BERKLEY PUBLISHING GROUP
TRASH TV SWEEPSTAKES
200 Madison Avenue, Dept. JJ
New York, New York 10016

NAME

ADDRESS

CITY   STATE   ZIP

Mail this entry form or a plain 3" x 5" piece of paper postmarked no later than July 14, 1997.

1. On an official entry form or a plain 3" x 5" piece of paper print or type you name, address, and telephone number and mail your entry to TRASH TV SWEEPSTAKES, THE BERKLEY PUBLISHING GROUP, DEPT. JJ, 200 Madison Avenue, New York, New York 10016. No purchase necessary.

2. Entries must be postmarked no later than July 14, 1997. Not responsible for lost or misdirected mail. Enter as often as you wish, but each entry must be mailed separately.

3. The winner will be determined in a random drawing on July 28, 1997. The winner will be notified by mail.

4. This drawing is open to all U.S. and Canadian (excluding Quebec) residents age 13 and over. If a resident of Canada is selected in the drawing, he or she may be required to correctly answer a skill question to claim a prize. Void where prohibited by law. Employees (and their families) of Penguin Putnam Inc., Pearson, plc and their respective affiliates, retailers, distributors, advertising, promotion and production agencies are not eligible.

5. Taxes are the sole responsibility of the prize-winner. The name and likeness of the winner may be used for promotional purposes. The winner will be required to sign and return a statement of eligibility and liability/promotional release within 14 days of notification.

6. No substitution of the prize is permitted. The prize is non-transferable.

7. In the event there is an insufficient number of entries, the sponsor reserves the right not to award the prize.

8. For the name of the prize-winner, send a self-addressed, stamped envelope to TRASH TV SWEEPSTAKES, Dept. JJ, The Berkley Publishing Group, 200 Madison Avenue, New York, NY 10016.